Coping with Alcohol Abuse

Janet Grosshandler

ROSEN PUBLISHING GROUP, INC. / NEW YORK

Published in 1990 by The Rosen Publishing Group, Inc.
29 East 21st Street, New York, NY 10010

Copyright 1990 by Janet Grosshandler   91- 1780 2

First Edition

Manufactured in the United States of America

Library of Congress Cataloging-in-Publication Data

Grosshandler, Janet.
    Coping with alcohol abuse / Janet Grosshandler.—1st ed.
        p.   cm.
    Includes bibliographical references and index.
    Summary: Provides, by examining family and peer environments which
foster alcohol abuse, coping skills to prevent such abuse and to
guide teenagers through counseling and recovery from alcoholism.
    ISBN 0-8239-1182-9
    1. Teenagers—United States—Alcohol use—Juvenile literature.
2. Alcoholism—United States—Prevention—Juvenile literature.
[1. Alcoholism.]   I. Title.
HV5066.G76   1990
362.29'2'0835—dc20

                                        52269   90-41102
                                                    CIP
                                                    AC

Manufactured in the United States of America

For my mother, Edna Holstein

A B O U T   T H E   A U T H O R ◇

Janet Grosshandler is a guidance counselor at Jackson Memorial High School, Jackson, New Jersey. Helping teenagers work through difficult problems in their lives has been a high priority in her life.

Janet earned her BA at Trenton State College in New Jersey and soon followed with an MEd from Trenton while teaching seventh-grade English. Working as a guidance counselor for thirteen years has given her a wide range of experience with adolescents. She also writes a weekly newspaper column, "Counselor's Corner," which advises teens and their parents on coping with the ups and downs of the teenage years.

Recently widowed, Janet lives with her three young sons, Nathan, Jeff, and Michael. She squeezes in time for running and reading.

Acknowledgments

I wish to thank the following people for their help in writing this book:

My sons Nate, Jeff, and Mike for sharing computer time with me;

My mother, Edna Holstein, who gives so much of herself to our family;

Rick and Nancy, Judy and Paul, Barbara and Don, and Arthur, for their super support;

Vickie Wilson (again!) for all the info, charts, books, pamphlets, and contacts;

The Rosen Publishing Group for these opportunities;

The Guidepost Ministries for the Iron Eyes Cody story.

My thanks and appreciation to all you teenagers who share your lives with me so that I can understand your realities and problems. I learn from you every day.

And it's important for me to mention here my husband, Hank, who died on April 28, 1989, from cancer. He made my life special and wonderful. I am what I am today because of his unconditional love and total support.

Some of the names in this book have been changed to protect the anonymity of the teenagers who were interviewed. A few are composite stories of two or three teens.

Contents

.

CHAPTER 1

Sherri's Story

"I was never much of a drinker," said sixteen-year-old Sherri. "Ugh, I hated the taste of beer, and most wine was too sicky-sweet."

So what was this high school junior doing in a rehabilitation program for teenage alcoholics and other drug abusers?

Sherri gave a sigh and pushed her long brown bangs out of her eyes. She avoided eye contact and spoke softly.

"You see, I used to be fat and I wanted to lose some weight. So I went on this starvation diet for a few weeks and lost fifteen pounds. I looked pretty good, and then I wanted to change my image. You know? Like get rid of the ugly fat girl and here comes the skinny, funny Sherri."

Sherri's friend turned her on to some of the "right" parties and to vodka and tonic. (Not so many calories as beer and pizza.) Sherri lost some of her inhibitions, picked up her first real boyfriend, and once and for all shed her "straight" image and took on her new "party girl" persona.

"I couldn't believe it when Roger started coming on to me. We were at this party at a real popular guy's house. There was a whole refrig full of wine coolers, a keg out back, and bottles of liquor all over the counter. I met Roger by the vodka, and he made me a drink. It was a pretty strong one, I think, but it wasn't my first of the night so I don't remember.

"Anyway, Roger and I danced a lot. He's a really good slow dancer, if you know what I mean, and he's a senior so I was feeling pretty lucky. Roger went outside a few times where some kids were passing around some joints, but I wasn't into that, so I stayed inside. But, you know, I was afraid he wouldn't come back to me when he came in, because there were lots of other girls there and he could have one of them.

"I met him at the back door as soon as he came in the last time so he wouldn't go off with someone else. We drank more and danced more, and he said he liked me and wanted to take me home. We went into one of the bedrooms for a while and things went farther than I should have let them, but it felt good to be with someone and fool around. I wasn't that drunk though, and I told him no when he wanted to have sex, but it was really hard. I wanted him to like me, you know?"

Sherri had promised her best friend, Lori, that she would go home with her. When she told Roger she couldn't go with him, he seemed to take it in stride and told her he hoped he would see her at another party the next night.

All the next day Sherri agonized over making arrangements to go to that party, lying to her parents about where it was and who was giving it. She talked to Lori on the phone six times about what she should wear so Roger would notice her and want to be with her again. Every time the phone rang, Sherri had to swallow her disappointment that it wasn't Roger calling.

"Hey, looking good, Sherri," that long-awaited voice whispered in her ear about ten o'clock that night.

It was Roger, breezing in late and a bit drunk, but he

was a welcome sight for Sherri, who had watched the door for the past hour as she downed three vodka and tonics.

Sherri and Roger danced a few times, but the party was so crowded that they didn't get to move around much. So much the better, because Roger was having a hard time standing up and leaned on Sherri most of the time. She didn't mind though, because he would whisper funny things in her ear and kiss her on the neck. It gave her chills up and down her spine.

When Roger suggested that they try to find an empty bedroom, Sherri was high enough and in love enough to do everything Roger wanted to do. She lost her virginity on top of a pile of coats in somebody's little brother's bedroom. It didn't even bother Sherri much when Roger got up right away to go throw up in the adjoining bathroom. Sherri was still flying from the loving, or was it the vodka?

Sherri and Roger became a couple, the answer to her dreams. They saw each other at school a little, but mainly the weekends were their time together because of Roger's after-school job. Sherri's romance settled into a pattern— Friday and Saturday nights he'd get a bottle of vodka for them to share. They usually went over to someone's house where the parents were out, or to Roger's older brother's apartment when no one was there.

They'd drink, watch TV, fool around, and end up having sex. Sherri felt loved and happy. She belonged to someone now, and he loved her.

The problems started when Roger lost his job.

Sherri looked up and for the first time pain showed in her eyes.

"The owner of the gas station accused him of stealing money. I didn't think Roger did it, but the guy fired him anyway. We had no money now for the weekends.

"I had to start taking beer and vodka from my house,

and then I stole money from our emergency fund in the cookie jar. Mom mentioned that she thought there was more in the jar when she had to buy a new tire for her car, but I just pretended I didn't know anything about it.

"I started taking baby-sitting jobs to get more money, and Roger would visit me after the kids were in bed. He'd drink whatever was in the house, but I was a little nervous about that and didn't drink much. Usually we'd have an argument depending on Roger's mood. I worried that he'd be there when the people got home, but he always left in the nick of time.

"All this went on for a few months, and my parents started pressuring me about Roger. They didn't like him very much, and they knew I had come home drunk a few times after being with him. My grades weren't as good as they used to be. But I thought, so what? Roger loves me, and I want to be with him no matter what my parents say.

"Only Roger started coming to school high. We cut out one lunchtime and went to his house. He had gotten some vodka, and we ended up in his bedroom all afternoon. He said he'd never had a girl in his room before and that I was special to him. He gave me his ring and I was so happy!"

Then the bottom fell out of Sherri's world. Her guidance counselor called her mother, concerned over Sherri's cutting school and getting poor grades. Her parents came down on her hard, grounded her, and forbade her to see Roger. Sherri cried, ranted and raved, and locked herself in her room the next Friday night.

Craving alcohol and wanting to be with Roger, Sherri climbed out her window and sneaked out. She combed the town looking for him, but to no avail. At two in the morning she went home, only to face her parents, who had discovered her open window and empty room.

"Now that I look back, my parents were trying to help

me. They knew I was in trouble even though I didn't see it for myself. But I wouldn't listen to anybody. Roger was my life, and I needed to be with him and drink with him to feel that my life was good."

Sherri tried to talk to Roger about not drinking so much. He wouldn't agree. In fact, he asked for his ring back since her parents weren't going to let her see him. Sherri told him everything was cool, and she continued to defy her parents by sneaking out for weekend binges of vodka and Roger.

"This is still really painful to talk about even now," Sherri's eyes filled with tears. "I guess Roger and I weren't very careful, since we were drunk most of the time, but I got pregnant. I told him right away because I was so scared. He freaked. I mean, really freaked. He called me stupid and said I should have been using something and that we'd have to do something about it fast.

"Roger borrowed money from his brother and gave it to me and told me to go have an abortion. At first I was in a state of shock. I thought he loved me, and now he was treating me like a problem he couldn't wait to get rid of.

"I didn't know what to do, but I knew I could never tell my father or mother. So I went to a clinic in the city and had an abortion. Roger drove me to the place and waited outside. When it was over we went to his brother's place, and he got drunk. All I could do was sit there and cry. For once I didn't drink. He got so mad at me, and we had this huge argument. He took his ring back and dropped me off at home.

"I'm not proud of this, but I was so depressed that night that I took a bottle of my mother's pills and drank a lot of vodka as I took them. See, I couldn't live without Roger and I couldn't live with what I had done about our baby. I wanted to die, so that's what I tried to do."

Sherri's parents found her and rushed her to the hospital. Her stomach was pumped and her life was saved. Sherri's alcohol abuse and secret abortion were revealed during all this. Her parents got help for her from the hospital's mental health specialists. Fortunately, Sherri was ready to start dealing with her growing addiction and depression.

"So here I am," Sherri said with a wry smile. "I guess I was pretty desperate, but this rehab place does a lot of counseling with us. We have group meetings all the time, and I'm getting help in understanding and dealing with my addiction to vodka and also my emotional dependence on Roger.

"The funny thing, though, all along I never thought I had an alcohol problem, and that turned out to be an underlying cause of everything else that went wrong. I never realized it until I wanted to kill myself and almost succeeded. This place is helping me get my life back together so I can face things without drinking and without using alcohol as an excuse to do everything else wrong that I did. It's a tough way to learn a lesson.

"But at least I'm alive to learn it."

CHAPTER 2

Introduction

"**W**asted."

"Ripped."

Hammered . . . blasted . . . wiped out . . . spent . . .

What did you get last weekend?

Drinking alcohol is the recreation of choice for many teens, especially on Friday and Saturday nights. Alcohol is the number one drug used and abused by teenagers in America. Recent statistics show that other drug use has declined slightly, but alcohol use still runs strong.

Parents even choose drinking for their kids over other dangerous activities.

"Look," said a father of three teenage sons, "when my kids drink, at least I know what it is, how it's made, and what to expect. You can't say that about pot, cocaine, or crack. I don't want them drunk, but I'd rather have them sneak a six-pack than snort coke."

Alcohol is familiar. Parents feel comfortable in their knowledge of how to deal with alcohol use and abuse rather than feel scared and helpless because they don't know how to help a daughter who's smoking crack.

Parents also set the example.

"Friday night has been beer and pizza night at my house for as long as I can remember," said Tammy, a teen who lives with an older brother and her father since her mother died six years ago. "I used to drink soda, but when I turned seventeen Dad said I could have beer too. Even though the drinking age in our state is twenty-one, my father feels it's okay because he's there with me. Besides, it's our house. We're not hurting anyone."

If your parents drink pretty regularly, chances are that you perceive that as "normal" and set your standards along those lines. Having "a few" before dinner and "celebrating" on the weekends becomes the norm in your life. However, by blowing off some heavy-duty pressure with some heavy-duty drinking, you could follow your parents' lead into alcohol abuse.

Many people in society see drinking alcohol as "okay," and obtaining beer and other liquor is not difficult for underage kids. It's usually available in everyone's refrigerator right next to the cola or diet soft drinks.

In this country, kids are starting to drink younger and younger, averaging right now at about thirteen years old. The greatest proportion of teenage drinkers are boys, but girls are drinking more and more too. Look around your class in school. Who do you think are the drinkers and alcohol abusers? With over 3.3 million teenage problem drinkers, you might be able to spot one or two right away.

"Mary Anne McCarthy always brags in homeroom on Monday mornings about how drunk she got over the weekend," Murf said. "It's like she's proud of it or something."

When Mary Anne talks, people listen. She likes it when she shocks the other kids with her outrageous behavior. So that kind of drinker is easy to spot. But what about the other drinkers sitting around your homeroom? Could you pick them out?

You might have suspicions about a few more, but many young drinkers hide their getting high very well. Breath mints, eyedrops, and lies cover up for the drinking and camouflage their growing dependence.

Most kids get their first taste of alcohol at home. The Thanksgiving "toast," champagne at a family wedding, sips from a parent's beer can or glass of wine, and sneaking a wine cooler at a barbecue are all familiar experiences.

Your parents' drinking habits will influence your own emerging alcohol habits, and research shows that if you begin drinking at an early age you are more likely to be a heavy drinker in your teen years and as an adult. Alcoholism, the disease of overdependence on alcohol, can develop quicker and require less alcohol for teens than for adults. Some kids become alcoholics in one to two years.

Weekly Reader, a magazine for elementary school children, conducted a survey among its readers and obtained some startling results. According to the poll, wine coolers, the alcohol industry's newest drink, were accepted by fourth-graders as "healthy fruit drinks." Only 24 percent of the kids thought that wine coolers were a drug. More than 74 percent thought that drinking one wine cooler a day was harmless. Wine cooler advertising has been pretty successful, hasn't it?

The fact is that these "harmless" wine coolers contain almost 5.5 percent alcohol, as much as beer. Kids who are beginning to experiment with alcohol find the fruity taste appealing, not bitter like beer.

LISTEN, a drug-prevention magazine, has labeled the wine cooler the newest "gateway" drink for kids because the sweet taste and attractive advertising make it more appealing and acceptable to people who are not used to drinking. Teens are switching to wine coolers from non-alcoholic drinks. Wine coolers are now competing with soda and fruit juices rather than the beer or wine market.

Abusing alcohol or having a drinking problem doesn't mean that you drink every day. But if you find yourself drinking more regularly and realize that you can't stop, then you have a problem. Drinking wine coolers, beer, and wine can be just as addictive as "hard" liquor such as vodka or whiskey.

Beer and wine are believed by many teens to contain less alcohol than other liquor. It's how you drink it that equalizes the alcohol intake. Look at the following table:

	Alcohol Content	Serving Size
Beer	4–5%	12 ounces
Wine cooler	5%	8 ounces
Wine	12–14%	4–5 ounces
Vodka and OJ	35–50%	one glass (1½ oz. of liquor)
Gin and tonic	35–50%	one glass (1½ oz. of liquor)

The above drinks are all equal in the amount of alcohol you consume.

Having one vodka and orange juice every night is the same as one beer a night. One 12-oz. can of beer equals one glass of wine equals one gin and tonic. Without realizing it, you could be considered a problem drinker by just downing a few beers a day. It depends on you, your tolerance, and your life situation.

Advertising companies do their best to make drinking seem attractive and the only way to go when you want to have fun. You can't watch a sports event on television without seeing an endless parade of former sports stars touting their favorite brand of beer.

How about those shots of the crowd at a major league baseball or football game? Those guys who took off their shirts in 15-degree weather at the Super Bowl and hammed it up for the camera sure looked like they were having a great time as they downed their fifth—or was it their sixth?—beer in the first half. Har, har! What a way to go!

Or how about those sexy ads in the magazines? According to the advertising companies, you can't have love and romance unless you drink before, during, and after.

"Well, drinking some wine does loosen me up," fifteen-year-old Patty said. "I feel happier and can flirt with the older guys at a party and have fun. I'd probably never do that sober."

The message that Patty gives when she drinks is different than when she is sober. Are these older guys attracted to Patty as she really is, or only when she's drunk and they can get her alone for a "good time"?

American children between the ages of two and eighteen see 100,000 TV commercials for beer, according to the National Council on Alcoholism. Add to that the newspaper and magazine ads, and kids are bombarded with the message "Drink! Drink! It's okay to drink! It's fun! Everyone does it!"

Beer remains advertising's favorite promotion, and teenagers are taking its direction younger and more often these days. Kids don't see beer or wine coolers as dangerous. Alcohol is acceptable in American families and is not always seen in the category in which it belongs—with drugs.

Getting "wasted" or "drunk out of my mind" is the goal of many a teenage weekend partier. It's not that kids get together and have a beer and some tacos before going to the Friday night movie. Drunkenness is the aim, and how fast seems to be a rule of this deadly game. And deadly it can get, because alcohol is a cause for a high percentage of teenage deaths in drunk driving accidents.

According to the National Institute on Alcohol Abuse and Alcoholism, teenagers who drink have a greater chance of moving on to other drugs and also of becoming heavy drinkers or alcoholics later on. Many kids are not aware of or don't seem to care about the frightening statistics of dependency and addiction that can result from alcohol use and abuse.

"Yeah, we got all that stuff in freshmen health class, but who really believes that all that really happens?" says Sandy, sixteen. "I mean, I go out, drink a six-pack, have some fun, and go home. No harm done, right?"

That's the outlook and opinion of a majority of teens and preteens. The "no harm done" mentality causes kids to be caught unaware when the dependence grows stronger and stronger on the "high" they get, and they begin to live their lives around their drinking. It's the most readily available and easiest drug upon which to become dependent, and getting off alcohol becomes harder and harder every day.

The teenage years are a time to separate from your parents and family and strike out on your own. You want to establish your own identity and life apart from Mom and Dad. Making your own mature decisions and calling all the shots become more and more important. Teens want to be grown-up.

Drinking is seen as an adult thing to do. Kids follow the role models set by their parents, older siblings, and friends. When the role modeling includes getting drunk every so often and including alcohol in many aspects of your life, some of those mature decision-making skills go right out the window. Teens who have been doing heavy-duty drinking for a few years are not always capable of making sensible decisions. Emotional growth and development are stunted by alcohol abuse.

How do you get a handle on this potential problem? How can you keep your friends, get invited to the "right" parties, and be popular if you don't drink? What can you do as you move along that rocky road to alcohol abuse? Is there a way out?

Being armed to the teeth with correct information is a good first step. Being aware of the risks involved and the strategies and skills necessary to keep your friends and stay sober can take you a long way along that road. And knowing where to get help and how to get help when you need help with your drinking can take you off that self-destructive alcoholic collision course you may be on.

This book is a start. You can make it through your teenage years sober and healthy. Growing up emotionally, physically, socially, and spiritually are all important components of a healthy adolescence. You can do it if you have the information and skills necessary for *Coping with Alcohol Abuse*.

CHAPTER ◇ 3

What Is Alcohol?

A lcohol has been around for a long time. Many hundreds of thousands of years ago, our ancestors mixed fruits, berries, honey, and other substances with water. When these mixtures were left in the sun, they were transformed into a fruity liquid that seemed to have special powers.

Our ancestors found that these potions could make them feel happy, relieve pain, and be useful for medicinal purposes. Use of the magic liquids became part of rituals and religious ceremonies.

On and on it went throughout history. Alcohol has been part of the life-style of the human race for ages. There is no time in recorded history when alcohol has not played a part.

But the part it has played has been a double-edged sword. One of the early American settlers, a Puritan clergyman named Increase Mather, said in 1673, "Drink is in itself a good creature of God, and to be received with thankfulness, but the abuse of drink is from Satan; the wine is from God, but the Drunkard is from the devil."

A Frenchman echoed the sentiment in the eighteenth

century. François de Salignac de La Mothe-Fenelon said, "Some of the most dreadful mischiefs that afflict mankind proceed from wine; it is the cause of disease, quarrels, sedition, idleness, aversion to labor, and every species of domestic disorder."

Even when the United States government outlawed the use of alcohol during the years of Prohibition (1919–1933), people drank.

Ethyl alcohol is the main ingredient in all the beers, wines, and other liquors you see lined up in the window of a liquor store or in your parents' liquor cabinet. It is what makes you drunk and damages your brain, liver, and other body organs.

Ethyl alcohol is created by a process called fermentation. The ethyl alcohol is excreted by the yeast fungus, which has an insatiable appetite for sweet things. When the yeast finds fruit, honey, potatoes, berries, or cereals, it gives off an enzyme that changes the sugar into carbon dioxide (CO_2) and alcohol. That is fermentation.

The yeast continues to cause fermentation until it dies. And it dies of intoxication or, you could say, drunkenness. Fermentation stops at different percentage levels, usually about 13 to 14 percent. In beer, which is made from cereals such as barley and corn, fermentation stops at about 3 to 6 percent alcohol, wine from 10 to 14 percent. The yeast can't take any more, so it dies.

Man discovered how to distill alcohol about 800 A.D. Distillation is removing the undissolved particles and leaving the concentrated alcohol, thereby increasing the alcohol content. By adapting temperature and time, distilled or "hard" liquors were created: whiskey, gin, rum, and others. The alcohol content in these liquors is anywhere from 40 to 75 percent.

On the label of a bottle of liquor the content of pure

alcohol is stated as "proof." In the seventeenth century, in order to "prove" that the alcohol was strong enough, some Englishmen mixed it with gunpowder and tried to set it on fire and explode it. If the drink contained almost 50 percent alcohol, it would ignite. So the "proof" is double the amount of pure alcohol: 100 proof whiskey contains 50 percent pure alcohol; 80 proof vodka is 40 percent pure alcohol.

The classification of alcohol as a drug may be a surprise to you. By definition it is a food, because it unites with oxygen (oxidizes) to produce energy and form carbon dioxide and water in your body. This process provides the body with calories in the same way that other food does.

The calories produced by alcohol, however, are empty calories, on the order of "junk food." Alcohol provides no protein, vitamins, or minerals. Since most alcohol comes from sugar, it adds unwanted calories to your daily intake. The other side of the coin is the way alcohol acts as a drug. Although it is not a prescription medicine or an illegal drug like cocaine, alcohol acts as a depressant on the central nervous system.

At first, alcohol acts as a stimulant. It gives you a buzz, makes you feel silly and less inhibited. That is because the alcohol acts on the part of your brain where are stored your learned behaviors such as self-control. So if you drink only a little and eat as you drink, you loosen up and seem to have a louder, funnier time than if you weren't drinking.

But the more you drink, the more you saturate your brain, and the drug-like effects of alcohol begin to depress your nervous system. You may still think you are having a good time, but your slurred speech and tipsy walk tell more than you know. Keep on drinking and you may pass out before you realize how much you've really had.

Be aware of what you take into your body. If you are at a

party, some one might push a glass in your hand and tell you to drink it. Unless you know what it is and what it can do to you, you are taking a risk by chugging it down in the name of "fun."

CHAPTER ◇ 4

Effects of Alcohol

"**T**hat first drink, when I down it real fast, gives me that buzz. You know, a happy, silly feeling. I can loosen up with my friends and have a good time," said Carla, sixteen.

"The only thing I don't like," she added, "is when kids can't control themselves. When some of the guys and even some girls drink too much, they break things at the party, or get in a fight, or puke all over the bathroom."

Drinking makes a person feel different. The alcohol works to relax you by slowly depressing your central nervous system. At first you may feel what you consider an enjoyable "high"—less inhibited, a little exhilarated, and funny.

Alcohol enters your bloodstream directly without being digested. Some researchers say that small amounts are absorbed directly through the lining of your mouth and throat, going straight to your brain. It goes through the walls of your stomach and small intestine and is absorbed into your blood. From there it travels directly to your brain. Your body burns off alcohol at a constant rate—about one ounce of 100 proof liquor an hour. If you drink more than you can eliminate, the drug accumulates in your body. You become intoxicated, meaning that the poisonous or *toxic* effects of alcohol go into action in your brain and in your body.

Five Stages of Intoxication

(This research is based on a 150-pound person. If you weigh less than that, check the charts on the following pages to find out the accurate rate for your weight.)

[One drink is defined as:
12 ounces of beer;
5 ounces of wine;
1 wine cooler;
1½ ounces
of hard liquor mixed in
a drink.]

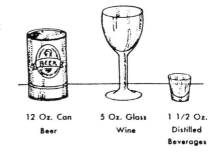

12 Oz. Can Beer   5 Oz. Glass Wine   1 1/2 Oz. Distilled Beverages

Alcohol is measured by calculating the blood alcohol Concentration, referred to as BAC. Dr. Gail Milgram, Director of Education and Training at the Center for Alcohol Studies, Rutgers University, defines BAC as "the term used to designate the amount of alcohol in a person's blood. The BAC is always written as a decimal part of 1 percent." A BAC of .10 means that you have one part alcohol to 1000 parts of blood in your body. It is the amount that would make you legally drunk.

Stage 1. You have two drinks within two hours. Your BAC reaches .05, which means that one part of alcohol is mixed with 2000 parts of your blood. You may feel "up," relaxed, talkative, sociable, and attractive to others.

Stage 2.   You drink another beer or two. Your BAC moves up to the .10 range (one part alcohol to 1000 parts blood). The alcohol that felt like a stimulant before becomes a depressant and begins to interfere with your brain activity. Your motor skills are affected. It's becoming fuzzier to think and your speech slurs. Your emotions can be slightly exaggerated, and your reaction time slows down.

Stage 3.   Having four or five drinks within two hours boosts your BAC up to .20, which impairs your brain's function considerably. You have difficulty with gross motor skills, making you stagger. Moodiness and depression can overcome your personality. Your judgment and memory are impaired. At this point you need six to eight hours without another drink to return to normal.

Stage 4.   Adding more drinks in two to four hours can raise your BAC to .30 (one part alcohol to 300 parts blood). You are in a drunken stupor, really out of it. You don't know what you're doing, and you exhibit irresponsible behavior. You can hardly walk, talk, or stand. All your physical and mental functions are seriously impaired.

Stage 5.   By drinking recklessly and uncontrollably within a short period of time, you can raise your BAC to .40 or .50 (one part alcohol to 250 or 200 parts blood). You are unconscious, blacked out, or in a coma. The part of your brain that controls your breathing is severely affected. Paralysis can grip your respiratory system and you can stop breathing. Death is not far away.

Usually teens stay within the first stage or two, although many kids say that if they are going to drink, they drink to get drunk.

By drinking enough to increase your BAC to dangerous levels you endanger your health, your life, and the lives of others, especially when you drink and drive. Your drinking affects all the skills necessary for safe driving. The following alcoholic effects can cause you to have a fatal accident.

- Alcohol affects vision. (When a fuzzy picture is sent to your brain, you can't interpret the traffic scene in front of you.)
- Alcohol affects eye focus. (Your eye muscle is hampered, and what you see is blurry.)
- Alcohol affects how much light enters your eye. (The pupils of your eyes take longer to constrict to keep out light when you drink. You can be semiblinded for several seconds as you drive.)
- Alcohol produces double vision. Which of the *two* cars coming at you do you react to? Which set of headlights should you veer away from?)
- Alcohol affects judgment of distance. (No coordinated picture is sent to your brain. Trying to pass the car in front of you and misjudging the distance causes accidents.)
- Alcohol affects peripheral vision. (Seeing objects, pedestrians, and other cars on your sides as you drive is important. The more you drink, the less you notice what is there.)
- Alcohol affects night vision. (Seeing in the dark is hard enough. Alcohol reduces your ability even more.)
- Alcohol affects driving time-sharing skills. (Many tasks and skills are needed to drive safely. The computer in your brain receives "input" from what you see and do as you drive. Drinking throws off

your mental coordination, and you are less able to do several things at once.)

- Alcohol affects tracking skills. (Tracking skills involve using the steering wheel to keep your car in the correct lane, make left turns, and negotiate turns.)
- Alcohol affects reaction time. (How quickly you respond to a situation is crucial in driving. When you drug your reaction skills with alcohol, you can't put it all together.)

When you get in a car, your chances of being in an accident are 1 in 7. When you get in a car slightly drunk or with a drunk driver, your chances shrink to 1 in 3. Choose your odds.

As you begin to drink more, you develop a tolerance to alcohol. That means that your brain's sensitivity to alcohol changes and allows you more drinks before you feel the effects. You "tolerate" higher levels. Dependence and addiction can soon follow.

Your weight also determines how much you are affected by what you drink. A guy of 180 pounds can drink more than his girlfriend who weighs 115. She will reach the higher levels of intoxication before he does.

How fast you drink affects your BAC. Check the charts on the following pages to compare your intoxication level with the number of drinks taken in a few hours. If you sip a few beers over four hours, you won't get as drunk as your date who chugs four in a row as soon as you get to the party.

Whether your stomach is empty or full can alter alcohol's effects. Compare the following charts.

Your mood when you drink, how much you can tolerate,

how tired you are, and how experienced at drinking you are can all result in different levels of intoxication.

Getting sober follows drinking and/or getting drunk. The *only* factor that brings sobriety is *time*. Nothing can speed up the process. Coffee, cold showers, a walk in crisp

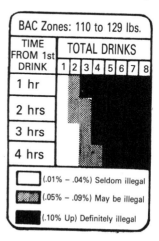

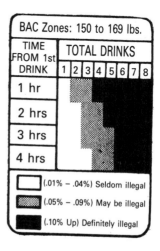

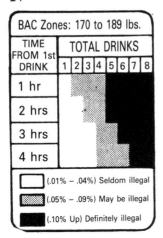

BAC Zones: 170 to 189 lbs.

TIME FROM 1st DRINK	TOTAL DRINKS							
	1	2	3	4	5	6	7	8
1 hr								
2 hrs								
3 hrs								
4 hrs								

(.01% – .04%) Seldom illegal
(.05% – .09%) May be illegal
(.10% Up) Definitely illegal

BAC Zones: 190 to 209 lbs.

TIME FROM 1st DRINK	TOTAL DRINKS							
	1	2	3	4	5	6	7	8
1 hr								
2 hrs								
3 hrs								
4 hrs								

(.01% – .04%) Seldom illegal
(.05% – .09%) May be illegal
(.10% Up) Definitely illegal

BAC Zones: 210 to 229 lbs.

TIME FROM 1st DRINK	TOTAL DRINKS							
	1	2	3	4	5	6	7	8
1 hr								
2 hrs								
3 hrs								
4 hrs								

(.01% – .04%) Seldom illegal
(.05% – .09%) May be illegal
(.10% Up) Definitely illegal

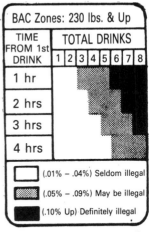

BAC Zones: 230 lbs. & Up

TIME FROM 1st DRINK	TOTAL DRINKS							
	1	2	3	4	5	6	7	8
1 hr								
2 hrs								
3 hrs								
4 hrs								

(.01% – .04%) Seldom illegal
(.05% – .09%) May be illegal
(.10% Up) Definitely illegal

air *do not* make you sober. The alcohol must be metabolized by your liver and work its way out of your body over a period of hours. That's the only "trick" that works.

There is no safe way to drive after drinking. The following charts show that a few drinks can make you an unsafe driver. They show that drinking affects your BAC. The

ESTIMATED AMOUNT OF 80 PROOF LIQUOR NEEDED TO REACH APPROXIMATE GIVEN LEVELS OF ALCOHOL IN THE BLOOD

"EMPTY STOMACH"
DURING A ONE-HOUR PERIOD
WITH LITTLE OR NO FOOD INTAKE PRIOR TO DRINKING

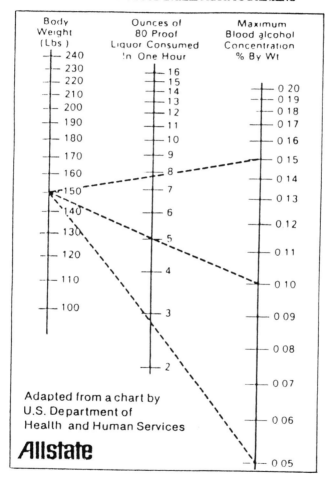

Adapted from a chart by
U.S. Department of
Health and Human Services

Allstate

Permission Granted by Dr. Marshall Stearn, author of *Drinking and Driving—Know Your Limits and Liabilities*, and Allstate.

"FULL STOMACH"
DURING A ONE-HOUR PERIOD OCCURRING BETWEEN ONE AND TWO HOURS AFTER AN AVERAGE MEAL

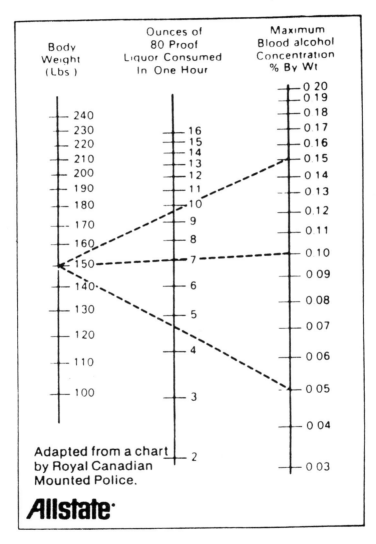

Adapted from a chart by Royal Canadian Mounted Police.

Allstate·

Permission Granted by Dr. Marshall Stearn, author of *Drinking and Driving—Know Your Limits and Liabilities,* and Allstate.

BAC zones for various numbers of drinks and time periods are printed in white, gray, and black. First, find the chart that includes your weight. For example, if you weigh 160 lbs., use the "150 to 169" chart. Then look under "Total Drinks" at the "2" on that chart. Now look below the "2" drinks, in the row for 1 hour. You'll see that your BAC is in the gray shaded zone. That means that if you drive after 2 drinks in 1 hour, you could be arrested. In the gray zone, your chances of having an accident are 5 times higher than if you had no drinks. If you had 4 drinks in 1 hour, your BAC would be in the black area . . . and your chances of having an accident 25 times higher. What's more, it is illegal to drive at this BAC (.10% or greater). Before reaching the white BAC zone again, the chart shows you would need 4 hours with no more drinks.

Long-term Effects of Alcohol

People who are heavy drinkers and alcoholics can develop serious physical and medical problems. The following have happened to real people, many of them teens, who thought, "Not me!":

Muscle disease and tremors.   Severe cramps in the muscles of the arms and legs is called alcoholic myopathy. After a while it becomes acute. The muscles swell and become weak; then follow twitching, tremors, and kidney failure.

Heart disease.   Continued heavy drinking directly affects your heart, causing it to pump less hard than when you were alcohol-free. Fatal heart attack can result because of the reduced oxygen.

Cirrhosis of the liver.   Your liver has the tough job of processing or metabolizing the alcohol that you drink. Heavy drinking causes destruction of the liver's cells until it can no longer do its job. Cirrhosis of the liver occurs about six times more often in heavy drinkers than in nondrinkers or very light drinkers.

Stomach problems. Preteens and teenagers are very susceptible to gastrointestinal irritation. Vomiting, indigestion, and diarrhea are the beginning signs, and it can progress to ulcers, gastritis, and pancreas inflammation.

Colds, infections, pneumonia. The more you drink, the more you lower your resistance to infections and infectious diseases. Your nutritional smarts go down the drain as you drink more and more, thereby reducing your body's strength to fight off viruses and bacteria.

These are among the short- and long-term effects of drinking. Does it seem as if all this is exaggerated? Some kids think it is just hype to scare you off of having "fun."

The truth is that all this is real and happens to real people. Go to a teenage detox ward in a hospital or to a rehab clinic and talk to those kids. They'll tell you how "real" it gets, how scary it gets, and how close to death many of them come.

Then decide for yourself whether it is all hype.

CHAPTER 5

Teenage Drinking
Habits

The National Adolescent School Health Survey was conducted in the fall of 1987. Approximately 11,000 eighth- and tenth-grade students from both public and private schools were polled. The survey asked questions about use of cigarettes, alcohol, and drugs and other social problems that adolescents meet.

The following information on alcohol use and abuse is highlighted from that survey. It is provided by the National Institute on Drug Abuse.

- 77 percent of eighth-grade students have tried alcohol, and of these, 55 percent report first trying it by grade six. 89 percent of tenth-grade students report having tried an alcoholic beverage; of these, 69 percent report first use by grade eight.
- 34 percent of eighth-grade students and 53 percent of tenth-graders report having had an alcoholic beverage during the past month.

- 26 percent of eighth-grade students and 38 percent of tenth-graders report having had five or more drinks on at least one occasion during the past two weeks.
- 13 percent of eighth-grade students and 18 percent of tenth-graders report having used a combination of alcohol and drugs on one or more occasions during the past month.
- 80 percent of the students surveyed perceive a moderate or great risk in the regular use of alcohol.
- 74 percent of the students report that their close friends would disapprove if they drank alcohol regularly; however, slightly less than half (43 percent) think that their close friends would disapprove if they drank alcohol occasionally.
- 84 percent report that it would be fairly easy for them to obtain alcohol.

In 1988 the Institute for Social Research at the University of Michigan (Ann Arbor) presented a cumulative survey called "Drinking and Driving Habits Among American High School Seniors."

The statistics for the survey were compiled by Patrick O'Malley, PhD, and Lloyd Johnston, PhD, for their Monitoring the Future Project. Across the nation over 17,000 high school seniors were polled about their drinking and driving habits.

DRINKING AND DRIVING AMONG AMERICAN HIGH SCHOOL SENIORS: EXTENT OF THE PROBLEM

Patrick M. O'Malley, PhD
Lloyd D. Johnston, PhD

Invited testimony presented at hearings before the
National Commission Against Drunk Driving and
National Highway Traffic Safety Administration
Fort Worth, Texas
March 29, 1988

	1984	1985	1986	1987
Prevalence of Alcohol Use, Past 30 Days:				
All Seniors	67.2	65.9	65.3	66.4
Prevalence of Five or More Drinks in a Row, Past Two Weeks:				
All Seniors	38.7	36.7	36.8	37.5
Percent Getting Drunk for First Time Before 10th Grade:				
All Seniors	—	—	38.2	38.2
Males	—	—	42.6	41.8
Females	—	—	34.4	34.7
Percent Driving More Than 50 Miles Per Week:				
All Seniors	41.8	43.5	45.0	47.9
Percent Driving After Drinking Alcohol:				
All Seniors	31.2	29.0	26.8	26.6
Males	39.2	36.6	33.9	33.3
Females	23.2	21.8	20.9	20.7

Percent Driving After Having Five or More Drinks:

All Seniors	18.3	16.6	15.8	15.0
Males	*25.2*	*24.0*	*22.6*	*22.2*
Females	*11.3*	*9.9*	*10.0*	*8.6*

Percent Riding as Passenger After Driver Had Been Drinking Alcohol:

All Seniors	44.2	39.1	38.2	38.2
Males	*43.5*	*38.9*	*37.2*	*39.4*
Females	*44.1*	*38.5*	*39.3*	*37.4*

Percent Riding as Passenger After Driver Had Five or More Drinks:

All Seniors	25.4	21.5	21.2	21.9
Males	*27.5*	*23.7*	*24.8*	*25.4*
Females	*22.6*	*19.3*	*18.2*	*19.0*

Percent of Seniors Using Seatbelts When Driving:

Never, Seldom	—	—	43.2	36.7
Always	—	—	25.0	33.0

Percent of Seniors Using Seatbelts When Riding as Passenger in Front Seat:

Never, Seldom	—	—	46.6	39.0
Always	—	—	22.0	30.1

Percent Reporting One or More Accidents in Past 12 Months:

All Seniors	22.8	24.4	25.1	25.6

Percent of Accidents After Alcohol Use (in Past 12 Months):

Accidents After Alcohol Use	12.1	11.1	8.8	9.7

Percent Reporting One or More Moving Violations in Past 12 Months:

All Seniors	26.5	27.6	30.4	31.7

Percent of Moving Violations After Alcohol Use (in Past 12 Months):

Violations After Alcohol Use	16.9	15.9	14.2	14.3

Friends' Disapproval of Drinking and Driving:

. . . After Having 1–2 drinks:

Disapprove	27.0	30.3	31.0	30.2
Strongly Disapprove	29.8	34.3	36.0	36.2

. . . After Having 5 or more drinks:

Disapprove	26.2	23.7	22.2	21.0
Strongly Disapprove	6.26	68.4	69.7	69.7

Permission granted, Institute for Social Research

These are the years when you are going to establish your habits. Where will you fall on the charts in the above surveys? What are your beliefs in regard to alcohol?

Teens and preteens run the gamut when it comes to what kind of drinkers they are. The following is a guideline upon which you can base your alcohol habits. Where do you fit in?

Comfortable abstainer

- Does not drink.
- Would not have alcohol no matter what the occasion.
- Can live with that decision comfortably.
- Is not forced into making decisions about alcohol.
- Not drinking is built into life-style.
- Other people accept this decision.
- Would not consider alternative decision.

- Does not fake it at parties with a glass of club soda or ginger ale.

Usual abstainer

- Mainly an abstainer, but does choose to drink on infrequent occasions.
- Life-style stays true to that of a basic abstainer.
- Decides to drink under certain circumstances.
- Could even drink excessively once or twice.
- May not drink for months or more than a year.
- May give in to pressure to have a drink or when he or she feels uncomfortable not drinking.
- Not always certain about the decision to abstain.

Light drinker

- Occasionally drinks.
- Limits self to very little alcohol.
- Does not drink on an empty stomach.
- Stops at one or two drinks.
- Life-style reflects decision to remain sober.
- Drinking is not an issue.
- Staying sober is the decision that sticks.
- May have alcohol in the house, but does not plan entertainment around drinking.
- Alcohol is not important.
- More a nonuser than a user.
- Considers self a drinker rather than an abstainer.

Frequent user

- Many occasions provide the opportunity to drink.
- Wants to reduce stress through alcohol escape.

- When everyone else is getting high, so is he or she.
- Does not consciously decide to drink and cause problems.
- Is aware enough not to drink and drive most times.
- Tries not to let alcohol interfere with school, family, or job.
- Likes to drink, to get high.
- Doesn't drink at school or at work.
- Still makes decisions based on not hurting anyone by drinking.
- Is responsible in relationships with other people.
- Doesn't feel guilty about drinking.
- May stick to one brand of beer or a certain type of drink.

Occasional abuser

- Drinks with the purpose of getting high.
- Places self in dangerous situations with drinking.
- Personally and socially goes out on the edge when drinking.
- Alcohol consumption affects others.
- Feels bad afterward.
- Starts having to deal with guilt.
- Is ashamed of behavior.
- Drinking may lead to antisocial behavior.
- Can remember what happened when drinking.
- May resolve to stop.
- Is living a life-style in which drinking is usually part of social occasions.
- Socializes with other drinkers.
- Can still make decisions about alcohol.
- May develop problems with family, school, job because of drinking.

- Still has control over alcohol.
- Has some health problems.

Alcoholic

- Drinks most of the time.
- If not drinking, is thinking about it.
- Is rarely sober.
- Control over alcohol is gone.
- Drinks compulsively.
- Can't make a rational decision because of alcohol.
- Health is deteriorating.
- Loses jobs, has problems at school because of drinking.
- Family is suffering because of him or her.
- May be involved in criminal activities or known to police.
- Won't go if there's no booze when socializing.
- Always having a supply of alcohol is most important.
- Cannot enjoy himself or herself unless drinking to excess.
- Does not think he or she has a problem.
- Is not at all interested in abstaining.
- Can't come up with reasons to stop.
- Drinking life-style is the only acceptable way to live.

Twenty questions for teenage drinkers

The following are questions that will help you self-diagnose your drinking habits. Few preteens and teens recognize outright that they have a problem. If you don't get drunk every night, there's no way you're an alcoholic, right? Wrong.

These questions are based on a similar questionnaire developed by the staff of Johns Hopkins University Hospital, in Baltimore, Maryland. The "Hopkins questions" were formulated to help young people identify alcoholism in their lives.

Be honest with yourself. No one will know how you respond to these questions except you.

1. Have you been absent from school or your part-time job because of drinking?
2. Do you drink to get high so that you can forget the fight you just had with your parent or escape from a family or school problem?
3. Is overcoming shyness with a drink important to you?
4. Are you alone or with friends when you drink?
5. Have your friends or the crowd you usually hang out with changed since you started drinking? Are you now in a "party animal" group?
6. Do your friends drink less than you do?
7. Have you lost friends because of your drinking? Is there someone who won't hang out with you now?
8. What is your reputation now? Has it changed since you have been drinking?
9. Are there people in your life (parents, teachers, friends, brothers, sisters) who tell you that you drink too much? Does that bother you?
10. Have you run into trouble at home or at school because of your drinking (being "caught," grounded, punished, etc.)?
11. Is your money going mainly into your drinking? Are you "borrowing" money or saving up your baby-sitting fees for that bottle of liquor?

12. Does drinking make you feel powerful, stronger, and more secure?
13. Do you have to take a drink or get high when you go out on a date?
14. Do you drink until the bottle is empty or the supply is gone? Do you drink whatever liquor you can get?
15. Do the guilts come on when you are drinking, or when you're coming off your high?
16. Do you drink to build up your self-confidence or to feel more comfortable around people?
17. Did you ever wake up and wonder what happened the night before?
18. Have you ever had to go to the hospital or been in trouble with the police because of your drinking?
19. When you get lectures and talks about alcohol abuse, do you blow them off?
20. Do you *think* you might have an alcohol problem that's not quite under control?

If you answered yes to just one question, it can be a warning sign that you're developing problems with your drinking. If you answered yes to any two questions, chances are that you are on the road to being an alcohol abuser. If you answered yes to three or more questions, you probably are an alcoholic.

CHAPTER 6

Why Drink?

"I want to have fun."
"My girlfriend likes me better when I'm high. She says I'm silly and funny."
"When I go to a party it's just the thing to do. You walk in the door and someone hands you a beer."
"I like to dance, and after I've had a few rum and colas I get a little crazier and dance better."

Teens and preteens try alcohol for a lot of reasons. The first time may be out of curiosity. You see your parents and other adults whom you respect "unwinding" with a scotch and water or having a bottle of wine on those "special" occasions. It seems part of the adult world. You want to be adult, so you imitate the adults you know.

Sometimes you start drinking because you are curious about the effects of alcohol. You've seen other kids who are high and seeming to have a "great" time. The movies and videos are full of party scenes and convince you that alcohol is harmless and a fun thing to try. So you give it a shot.

Real friends introduce you to drinking, right? They've

got the six-pack and will leave you out if you don't come along and drink. How can you say no?

Everyone has a funny drinking story to tell about a memorable night of "eternal partying" or how someone made a complete fool of himself and how hilarious it was.

Remember when Larry Martin crawled up the steps to the school to buy a ticket for the dance and passed out at the ticket booth?

Or when Angie Putnam polished off that pint of vodka on the ski trip and tried to ski down the expert slope when she hadn't even mastered the bunny hill? Ha ha, way to go, Angie.

Who can forget last month at the senior prom when Richie Rubens pushed the lead singer away from the microphone and started belting out a song in his off-key voice? Outasite, Richie!

Who has the funniest story? Doesn't everyone laugh at these hysterical stunts?

Do you think Larry's date laughed when all her friends saw that she was stuck with a drunk outside the dance?

Or maybe it was the teacher in charge of the ski trip who laughed the hardest when he had to call Angie's parents from the hospital. Falling off the ski lift and splitting her chin open sure was a crazy stunt.

Or do you think the lead singer in that group had a good laugh after Richie vomited all over his thousands of dollars worth of speaker equipment?

Sobering thoughts? Not to Larry, Angie, or Richie, who were successful in continuing their "outrageously funny" behavior. Unfortunately, they forgot that drinking has consequences. What you do affects other people.

Give yourself a quick test. Which of the following do you see as acceptable reasons for drinking? Choose as many as you wish.

Get "high" and feel good
Family celebration
Fear
Taste
Relieve anxiety
Excitement
To deal with a problem
Tradition
Confusion
Guilt
Being ashamed
On a dare
To be one of the crowd
When you feel hurt
Feeling uncomfortable

Peer pressure
Curiosity
To relax
Rebellion
For courage
Religious occasions
To relieve pain
To feel mature
Embarrassment
Feeling mixed-up
Just in the mood
To be different
When angry
Being shy
When worried

Marcy feels bored. "What else is there to do in this hick town anyway? Give me a drink."

James's girlfriend just dumped him. "There's Connie with her new boyfriend. I hope he can take it when she dumps him too. Pass me another beer."

Louis doesn't have many friends. "Another Friday night and I'm stuck here at home. I wonder if Dad finished off that gin yet."

Karen echoes her executive-type mother. "Jeez, I had a tough day. I need a drink."

Bobby can't shake his depression. "Life sucks. Get me a bottle, will ya?"

Holly hates her parents. "If they don't stop criticizing me, I'm going to run away. Split that bottle of wine with me, okay?"

Nancy's father split with another woman, leaving her mother with no money and a mess of bills to pay. "Now my parents will probably be getting a divorce. Who's gonna pay for that? I'm swiping the bourbon my dad left. He doesn't deserve to have it. I do."

Steve knows he can handle alcohol. "Look, I'm just drinking a little. No sweat. I can stop when I have to."

Every kid who drinks has a reason for doing it. Some sound legit. Others are just excuses. Evan's reason for drinking was tied up with his sexuality.

"I was tired of being an eighteen-year-old virgin. Listening to the other guys, I felt I was the last one on earth. So I started drinking at parties and getting high enough to pick up a few girls. I got to be pretty popular at parties and in the back seat of my car too."

For Evan, losing his inhibitions was important. How else could he give himself permission to experiment with sex. After all, *everyone* else is doing it, aren't they? Aren't teens supposed to try out sexual things? Isn't it cool to pick someone up, not really knowing or caring who she or he is, and get hot and heavy. Doesn't it make you cool? Aren't you grown-up now?

What do you think about yourself the next morning when you wake up trying to remember exactly what you did the night before?

Looking that hard for love sometimes stems from feeling unloved at home or by the opposite sex. Drinking seems to help you lose your inhibitions, but as you continue to drink the decision-making part of your brain gets fuzzy and you make the wrong decision or no decision at all.

Don't let a hot date turn into a due date. Sex and alcohol sometimes mix to make a baby. There heavy-duty consequences for those few minutes when you are high and looking for love.

A continuum of drinking is outlined below.

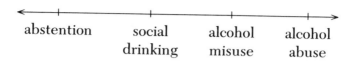

abstention   social   alcohol   alcohol
           drinking   misuse   abuse

From abstention to social drinking is certainly the safest life area in which to be. Social drinking involves slow, recreational consumption of alcohol as part of a family gathering or a special event. There are not many negative consequences when you have a glass or two of wine at your sister's wedding.

Alcohol misuse moves you into an area where there are obvious symptoms. It is usually done infrequently.

Alcohol abuse, at the far end of the continuum, is similar to misuse except that it occurs regularly. You move into the problem drinking and alcoholic areas here.

Where you fit on the continuum varies as you progress from childhood into your teen years. One thing is sure: You all start on the abstaining side. What would make *you* move along that line toward abuse? If you do, you'll jeopardize the physical, mental, and emotional aspects of your life.

Moving from childhood to adulthood brings enormous changes and important transitions. You seek independence and adult status. You struggle to gain control of your own life, and you experiment with new behaviors to see if they fit the emerging adult "you."

Why Not Drink?

"I made a promise to my parents. The car is mine as long as I don't drink. I don't want to lose the car."

"My cousin was killed in a car crash when her boyfriend was drinking and driving. I don't ever want to get within a thousand feet of that kind of situation."

"My brother went from smoking cigarettes, to drinking, to smoking pot, to cocaine. He's in a rehab now. If I drank, my parents would kill me. Plus I never want to end up the way he did. He almost destroyed our family."

"I don't like the taste. That's for real."

"I've seen kids passing out and lying on the floor in the middle of a party. I *never* want that to happen to me."

"I've decided that I want to be healthy. The kids I know who drink aren't healthy. They live to drink. That's not for me."

"I just don't. That's all."

For as many reasons you can give to drink there are just as many *not* to drink. The hard part is not going along with your crowd when it seems as if everyone is doing it.

Knowing the dangers, the consequences, and avoiding situations where you'll feel forced to drink can help you make the decision to keep off the bottle.

It can be simple.

The next time someone offers you a beer and asks, "Why not?" you can answer "Why?"

Chances are you won't get a very good reason.

CHAPTER ◇ 7

Alcoholic Scenarios

Responsible drinking involves deliberate decision-making. Trying to decide on the best and safest course of action quickly or while your friends are waiting for you to decide in two seconds isn't easy.

Weighing the consequences of your actions takes time and thought. Do you give in to impulsive decisions? You may never have been in this situation and have no experience on which to draw.

In order for you to give yourself some practice in deciding about alcohol, here are some scenarios in which you might become involved. Open-ended questions follow each fantasy situation to give you the opportunity to test out and practice your alcohol decision-making skills.

It would be nice if there were only one "right" answer or action that always worked in each situation, but that's not usually the case. Much is left up to you here, just as it will be when you go out this Saturday night.

Scenario #1

Your parents have to visit your grandmother overnight. They will be out of town on Friday night. Mom and Dad give their forty lectures about not having kids over and *no parties*!

You get permission for your best friend to spend the night. You have the pizza delivered and settle down to watch a movie. Your friend swipes a beer from the fridge. Before you can say anything, the doorbell rings. There stand six other kids from your English class.

"Hey, heard you needed some company tonight," Mark says. You glare over at your friend on the couch, who grins sheepishly.

- What's your instant reaction?
- How do you explain to your friends at the door that they can't come in?
- Do you tell them they can't come in?
- What are your feelings for your best friend who's finishing off the can of beer? Was it he who told the others?
- What choices do you have? Can you think of at least three?
- What would your parents think?
- What happens if other kids show up too?

Scenario #2

You had a minor role in the school production of *Grease*. The final performance makes you feel exhilarated but sad at the same time because you know that this great group of kids you've been with for hours every day will break up.

You are especially disappointed that the guy you have a crush on hasn't discovered you're alive yet. You have one more chance to get his attention—tonight at the cast party.

The party is at Ted's house. When you walk in you dive

into the mounds of food heaped on the kitchen table. You look in the fridge for something to drink. There's tons of soda and tons of beer.

- Were you planning on drinking tonight?
- Will drinking help with your sad feelings about the group's breaking up?
- Do you need to drink to get courage to catch "his" attention for the last chance?
- As you reach in the fridge, which can do you grab?
- What are the other kids doing? Does it matter if others are drinking or not?
- If everyone has beers, does that help you make the decision on what to drink?
- What kind of impression do you want to make on "him," and how do you make it?

Scenario #3

Your girlfriend got really drunk at a party. You didn't touch a drop. You want to get her home. As she trips up the steps to her house, the door swings open and there stands her father looking at you accusingly.

- What do you say to her father?
- Did you have any influence on her drinking?
- What do you do if her parents blame you for her condition and threaten to call your parents?
- Have a pretend discussion with your parents about this situation. What would you say? How would they react? In real life, could you have that kind of conversation with them?
- What about your girlfriend? Do you still want to see her?

- What are her drinking habits, and how do they affect you?
- Can you change her?
- Do you usually drink with her?
- Is drinking a big part of your relationship?

Scenario #4

Your mother just announced that she and your father are separating. You knew they had been fighting, but this comes as a shock. Your dad stops by to pack his clothes, and they have another rip-roaring argument.

You run out, jump in your car, and take off. You can't stand the tension anymore.

- Where do you go?
- When you get there, what do you do?
- If you end up at someone's house and they offer you a drink to chill out, do you take it?
- Does getting drunk sound like a good idea?
- Will it blot out the pain and confusion?
- What other choices do you have to deal with the hurt that this separation will bring into your life?
- How do you feel?

Scenario #5

You are invited to stay over at a friend's house. You thought it would be the regular gang, but two new kids were invited to this sleep-over. They show up with a hidden bottle of vodka.

You've never had anything more than a taste of your mother's wine. All the others are excited about having a "party" and are already filling glasses with orange juice to mix with the vodka.

"Where's your glass?" you are asked.

- Is the OJ in your hand?
- Are you interested enough to try it?
- What happens when the two new kids call you "chicken" if you hesitate about sharing the bottle?
- What do you know about the effects of finishing off a fifth of vodka among five kids?
- What do you do?

Scenario #6

You just got home from school dead tired. All you want to do is flop on your bed, put on your earphones, and doze for a while before your mother comes home from work in a couple of hours.

As you open the front door you know your plans will have to change. There in the kitchen sit your older sister, her boyfriend, and two other boys. The beer cans are piled high on the table, and the music is blaring.

- How do you view this situation?
- Are you the if-you-can't-beat-'em-join-'em type of person?
- What responsibility is it of yours what happens in that kitchen?
- What do you do about it?
- When your sister's boyfriend pulls you over and makes you sit next to him so he can "get to know you better," what do you say to him?
- Your mom walks in early and glares at you and your sister. What do you say?

Scenario #7

Your boyfriend urges you to drink more with him every time you go out. It does get sexier if you are both a little high, but you are afraid of doing too much. Lately it seems that the more you drink, the more sexually involved you get.

- How much of a part does drinking play in your relationship?
- Would it survive if you didn't drink?
- Can you stop drinking?
- How can you change your relationship so that you do things sober rather than drunk?
- Are you happy with yourself the next morning when you think about how you spent last night?
- Can you remember what you did last night?
- What do you think about as you get ready to go out with him the next time?

Scenario #8

You and your friend are hired to baby-sit for your father's boss's kids on the night of the company's Christmas party. After the kids are finally asleep, your friend Nickie says, "It's about time. Let's do it!"

The "it" she is talking about is raiding the very full liquor cabinets behind the wet bar in the family room. "There's so much here, no one will ever miss a few bottles," she says as she opens the first one.

- What is the first thing you say to her?
- As you see all the liquor in front of you, what are your impressions of your father's boss?

- As Nickie pours a strong rum and cola, what is your next move?
- What would happen to you if your parents found out?
- Nickie gets really drunk. What is your next move?
- Whom would you summon for help, or would you let her fend for herself?
- Your parents and his boss come home while Nickie is throwing up in the bathroom. What happens then?

Scenario #9

You are finally allowed to go to a party with your friends. When you get there, a keg is set up in the backyard for those who want beer. Other kids are sneaking out to the garage to smoke pot or do cocaine.

- What were you expecting at this party? Does this setup surprise you?
- Whatever you decide to do will be followed by your best friend, who does everything you do. Sometimes that bothers you. How do you feel about it tonight?
- You stay at the party. Where do you spend your time? In the house? Out back with the keg? In the garage?
- Do your parents know what kind of party this is? Do they care?
- Have you talked to your parents about these kinds of decisions? Do they trust you?
- What do you tell them the next morning at breakfast when they ask how the party was?

Scenario #10

You go into your younger brother's room to borrow some homework paper. In his desk drawer you find a half-empty pint bottle of vodka. He's only eleven.

- What are your first thoughts?
- How would you approach him about what you discovered?
- Would you approach him?
- Where do you turn to talk to someone about this?
- Do you just mind your own business?
- What would your parents do if you told them?
- How would your brother react if you told your parents?
- Is it up to you to do something?

When you wrestle with the questions presented above, part of the answers and solutions are tied up with how you feel about yourself. If you believe in yourself and value your health and life, that will influence your decisions. Kids with low self-esteem who are confused about who they are and feel that they aren't worthwhile sometimes make decisions that aren't healthy (physically and emotionally) for themselves. If you let others influence you and call all the shots, your life will be under the control of others who don't have your best interests in mind.

Work on strengthening your refusal skills and make plans that don't include alcohol. Here are some suggested responses.

"Instead of sitting in your garage getting high, I want to go to the mall."

"No thanks, beer and my stomach just don't mix."

"Let's leave this party now. It's getting out of hand."

"I'm working on more trust and freedom from my parents. If I go home drunk I'll be back where I was a year ago."

"Nope, I don't drink."

"I'd really like us to spend time together without drinking. How about we go roller skating Sunday night instead of to your friend's apartment?"

"I'm not drinking tonight."

"I'm hungry more than thirsty."

"Let's eat and skip the drinks."

"I'm the designated driver tonight. No drinking for me, thanks."

"I don't like that stuff."

You can use whatever variations you choose to keep yourself sober and safe. People go through a lot of changes when they drink. They become different physically, emotionally, mentally, and socially. Is that what you want for yourself?

CHAPTER 8

Party Tips

"**K**eys! Keys! Keys! That's what most people concentrate on at a party—take away everyone's keys," Joanie, seventeen, said. "It's like everyone has permission to get wasted as long as they hand in their car keys."

"But then who determines who gets their keys back?" she asked. "Usually it's another drunk kid who thinks he's not so drunk. Sometimes it's a parent."

If one point is getting across to teens and adults alike, it is, "Don't drink and drive." Drunken driving fatalities have shown a slight decrease over the past year or two. That may be an indication that the strong media campaigns are working. Some experts in the field say it's too soon to tell whether it is the beginning of a downward trend.

But doesn't that message have a two-sided view, as Joanie says? As long as you don't drive, is it okay to get bombed?

"Look," Patty said heatedly, "kids are going to drink. Almost all the adults I know drink. They party a lot too.

And they did it when they were teenagers. We just need to be a little careful. That's all."

As Patty says, teens will drink. It's naive to think that at some point all kids will decide never to touch a drop of alcohol again. So here are some "party" tips to be aware of and use to keep yourself as safe and sober as possible.

Whether the party is at your house or in someone's car, heeding the following can help you reduce the risks you take when you and your friends drink.

Your Weight

If you weigh 170 lbs. and your girlfriend weighs 110, it will take a lot less liquor for her to get drunk (see charts on pp. 23–24).

Every time Kenny emptied his beer can, he brought Katie one too. At first she tried to keep up, but because he weighed 60 pounds more, she got filled up, woozy, and nauseated while he seemed fine. Then Kenny got angry at her for "being such a lush."

Katie needs to know that she doesn't have to "keep up" with Kenny. It's okay to nurse one beer for a long time rather than rush to gulp a few down.

What You Eat

Eat. Eat. Eat. Take advantage of those party snacks (cheese and crackers, veggies and dip, pretzels) or have a nutritious meal beforehand. The fuller your stomach, the less you'll experience the effects of alcohol that you drink.

Food slows down the process by which the beer or wine is absorbed into your bloodstream. Since you don't feel high until the alcohol gets into your bloodstream, eating beforehand will keep your head clearer so you can make wiser decisions.

"Whenever I drink on an empty stomach, I get drunk right away," said Billy, sixteen. "Actually I get more sick than anything. I get a hot flush and feel light-headed for a while. That's not too bad. By the time I try to eat, I start feeling sick. One time my friends left me heaving my guts out in the diner parking lot. I guess they didn't want me throwing up in their car. It was kind of embarrassing.

"Now I make sure I eat first. Then I don't get that rush and I'm more in control of what I do."

Number of Drinks*	Blood Alcohol Concentration	Effects of Alcohol	Time to Leave the Body
1 or 1 or 1	0.03%	Relaxed; slight feeling of exhilaration	2 hours
2 or 2 or 2	0.06%	Slowed reaction time; poor muscle control; slurred speech; legs wobbling	4 hours
3 or 3 or 3	0.09%	Judgment clouded; inhibitions and self-restraint lessened; ability to reason and make logical decisions impaired	6 hours
4 or 4 or 4	0.12%	Vision blurred; unclear speech; stumbles when walking; hands do not work well together	8 hours

Number of Drinks*	Blood Alcohol Concentration	Effects of Alcohol	Time to Leave the Body
5 or 5 or 5	0.15%	All behavior affected; unable to remove clothes; staggers when walking without help; bumps into objects; drops things; activity requiring coordination cannot be performed; difficulty staying awake	10 hours

*Each drink contains 1½ ounces of whisky, gin, or other distilled spirit, or 5 ounces of wine, or 12 ounces of beer.

How Much You Drink

The more you drink over a short period of time, the more obviously you'll exhibit the effects of alcohol. Check out the chart. The time it takes for the alcohol to leave your body is important for you to know. Chugging four cans of beer in an hour may make you the life of the party for about ten minutes. Once that alcohol hits your bloodstream and travels through your body, your slurred speech and stumbling walk will get you as far as the couch, where you'll probably spend the rest of the party trying to sit up.

What You Are Drinking

12 oz. can of beer
5 oz. glass of wine
1½ oz. of distilled liquor

If the above are served in appropriate glasses, the amount of alcohol in the drinks and its effects are equal. However, if you pour four oz. of vodka and one ounce of OJ into the wine glass, you'll obviously increase the amount of alcohol and its effects on your body.

Length of Time

Gulping down your drinks because you are thirsty gets you started on the fast track to inebriation. Remember that alcohol is a drug and that overloading your body with this drug puts you at a disadvantage. Consuming four drinks over six to eight hours will keep you in control. Belting down four drinks in an hour and a half will probably put you out of commission.

Your Mood

How you feel emotionally and how you expect to feel when you drink can determine how drunk you get. Moody, tense people may drink faster and experience the effects of alcohol faster than those who are relaxed. If you expect that getting high will make you feel better and you don't, you may fall into a more depressed mood and grab another drink or two in an effort to blot it out.

Use a positive approach to drinking. "I can have a good time without bingeing. I don't need to get drunk to have fun. Staying in control and sober can keep me 'up'!"

What Kind of Fun Are You Looking For?

What's your goal for a successful evening? Is enjoying friends and meeting new people what you're looking for? Are you trying to impress that new girl who transferred in from Florida? Is this your first date with someone that you've had a crush on for a long time?

Getting smashed out of your mind can cause problems if your idea of fun is to bring about a happy ending to an enjoyable night.

Josh blew his first and only chance with a girl who had said no three times before she finally agreed to go out with him.

"I was real nervous, so I drank a little too much. When I took her home and was getting ready to kiss her goodnight, I lost my balance because I was a little drunk. I fell right off the front steps and into her mother's flowers." Josh grimaced at the memory. "She never went out with me again. I really blew it."

Stop Drinking an Hour Before You Leave

"One for the road" may be the one that makes you a statistic for fatal car crashes in your town. It takes about 15 to 20 minutes for the entire drink to be absorbed into the bloodstream and for you to feel its effects. You may feel sober enough to drive, but gulping down one more before you walk out the door may make your head swim in the middle of driving home.

Don't Drink and Drive or Ride with Someone Who Has Been Drinking

When you get into a car, your chances of being in an accident are one in seven. When you get in a car drunk or with someone who is driving drunk, your chances drop to one in three. The only way to deal with this is to be overcautious. Stay overnight, get someone else to drive, or have a contract with your parent to pick you up.

Don't make it an ego trip with, "Don't tell me I'm too drunk to drive. I know when I can drive or not." Be safe.

BREATH ALCOHOL CONTENT AND ITS EFFECTS

Drinks** In Body	APPROXIMATE BREATH ALCOHOL CONCENTRATION (In Grams*) Body Weight in Pounds								Effects on Feeling and Behavior	Effects on Driving Ability
	100	120	140	160	180	200	220	240		
1	.04	.03	.03	.03	.02	.02	.02	.02	Absence of observable effects. Mild alteration of feelings, slight intensification of existing moods.	Mild changes. Most drivers seem a bit moody. Bad driving habits slightly pronounced.
2	.08	.06	.05	.05	.04	.04	.03	.03		
3	.11	.09	.08	.07	.06	.06	.05	.05	Feeling of relaxation. Mild sedation. Exaggeration of emotions and behavior.	Drivers take too long to decide and act. Motor skills (such as braking) are impaired. Reaction time is increased.
4	.15	.12	.11	.09	.08	.08	.07	.06		
5	.19	.16	.13	.12	.11	.09	.09	.08	Slight impairment of motor skills. Increase in reaction time.	
6	.23	.19	.16	.14	.13	.11	.10	.09	Difficulty performing gross motor skills. Uncoordinated	Judgment seriously affected. Physical and mental
7	.26	.22	.19	.16	.15	.13	.12	.11		

Drinks**									Effects
8	.30	.25	.21	.19	.17	.15	.14	.13	behavior. Definite impairment of mental abilities, judgment, and memory. / coordination impaired. Physical difficulty in driving a vehicle.
9	.34	.28	.24	.21	.19	.17	.15	.14	
10	.38	.31	.27	.23	.21	.19	.17	.16	Major impairment of all physical and mental functions. Irresponsible behavior. Euphoria. Some difficulty standing, walking, and talking. / Distortion of all perception and judgment. Driving erratic. Driver in a daze.
11		.40	.34	.30	.27	.24	.22	.20	
12			.38	.33	.29	.26	.24	.22	
13			.40	.36	.32	.29	.26	.24	At .40, most people have passed out. Hospitalization is probable at BACs of .40 and above, and death is imminent. / It is hoped that the driver passed out before trying to get into vehicle.
14				.38	.34	.31	.28	.26	
15					.37	.33	.30	.28	

*Alcohol concentration is expressed here as grams of alcohol per 210 liters of breath. A reading of ".10" on a breath-testing instrument indicates 10 one-hundredths (10/100) grams of alcohol per 210 liters of breath.

**A drink is defined as: 1½ oz. of 80 proof liquor or 12 oz. of beer or 5 oz. of table wine. Subtract one drink, from the number consumed, for each hour of drinking after the first hour.

CHAPTER ◇ 9

Double Trouble

"If you open our medicine cabinet at home," said Reba, fifteen, "all these little bottles fall out. It's like the American bathroom isn't complete without drugs of all kinds."

The American culture seems to support the premise that popping a pill or taking medicine is the answer to whatever ails us. The adults are in charge of handing out the "medicine," and some people indiscriminately ingest quite a variety and amount of drugs every day. But these are not "drugs." It's really medicine, isn't it?

When we talk about real "drugs," most people assume that we mean the hard-core illegal substances that people take, sell, go to jail for, and sometimes die from. Actually any chemical substance that alters your behavior or the way you function is a drug. That usually means drugs you take for a desired result, such as antibiotics to get rid of an infection, but it has been extended to include things like insecticides and additives to liquids and food.

Think about this: You get up one morning and feel a cold coming on. You have a date tonight with that cute kid in your math class and you want to feel your best. So you stagger to the bathroom and presto! Right in front of you are the answers to your problem. You take some aspirin, slosh down some cough medicine for that tickly feeling in your throat, and put some drops in your eyes to get the red out.

Then you trudge downstairs to the kitchen and drink two cups of coffee with artificial sweetener and powdered dairy creamer. A little later your stomach feels queasy so you take a few antacid pills and then suck on several lozenges because your throat is still scratchy. Now didn't you take good care of yourself today?

With all that "medicine" and some rest, you're ready to party tonight! You and your date make it to the hottest dance club around and have a really good time. On the way home, after you have popped a few more cold tablets, you finish off with some beers at your friend's house. No harm, right? Then why do you feel so sick? Nauseated?

Guess what? You've ventured into the area of "double trouble"—mixing drugs and drinks. The instant remedies that line the shelves in the drugstores and the super-markets are supposed to give fast relief. Some of the labels have warnings: "Do not take this product if you are taking another medication."

Too bad the liquor bottle label or that six-pack of beer failed to warn you not to mix booze with other drugs. And liquor is a drug—the most accessible and frequently used drug around. Many people like to forget that fact. They hesitate to mix their drinks but think nothing of dosing up on antihistamine and then getting drunk before they've eaten dinner.

The following information comes from the U.S. Department of Health and Human Services.

When you take more than one drug you may experience "drug interaction." That means that one of the drugs in your body will change or alter the effects of the other drug. You might be lucky and mix drugs that don't interact with each other. Or you could be taking a big risk with your health and your life without being aware of the danger or the harm you are doing to your body.

The Department has broken down the interaction of drugs into four categories:

1. The drugs that you take together may act independently of each other.

For example, when you have bronchitis your doctor may tell you to take aspirin or acetaminophin to bring down your fever in addition to antibiotics to cure the infection in your system.

Some people take their vitamins at night with dinner. If you then have a few drinks, the effects of these drugs do not interact. They work independently in your body.

2. Drugs taken together may have an additive or summative effect.

In arithmetic class when you add 1 + 1 you get 2. That's the sum or the result of the addition. If you take two drugs that bring about the same result, you get twice the result.

For instance, you have a bad cough and you take some cough syrup containing codeine. The codeine is intended to put you to sleep or sedate your body, mind, and cough so you can sleep or rest. Drinking a lot of wine will also sedate you and make you sleepy. If you add the two together, you may just sedate yourself out right in the middle of dinner.

3. Drugs taken together may have a synergistic effect.

When you combine two drugs, the end result can be more than $1 + 1 = 2$. Synergism means that the total effect of the two drugs is greater than the summative effect mentioned above. One of the drugs increases the effect of the other drug. Drug A causes drug B to be intensified in its effect on your body, and the time your body reacts may be longer.

If you pop a few antihistamines for your cold and then drink, the two drugs have a synergistic effect. More sedation is produced. Sort of like $1 + 1 = 3$.

4. Drugs taken together may have an antagonistic effect.

Sometimes when you combine two drugs the total effect is less than if you took each one separately. For example, if you took an amphetamine and started drinking, your central nervous system would be less depressed than if you were drinking alcohol by itself. Sort of like $1 + 1 = 1\frac{1}{2}$.

That doesn't mean that it's safer to combine amphetamines and alcohol, because some drugs have more than one effect. While one effect may lessen the action of another drug, a second effect can occur independently. For instance, although the amphetamine lessens the depressant action of alcohol, it does not affect the loss of motor coordination that results from drinking too much. So you may feel more alert by popping some speed after drinking, but your driving skills still are impaired. You may think you are sober enough to drive, but the truth is that you are a potential killer behind the wheel of a car.

Some prescription and over-the-counter drugs when

mixed with alcohol can really endanger your health. The combination of liquor with certain drugs produces a toxic effect that can have serious consequences.

According to the Department of Health and Human Services the following drugs can interact to produce toxic effects in your body:

- *Alcohol and barbiturates*
  Did Elvis do it? Did Karen Ann Quinlan do it? Probably the most deadly combination of drugs is drinking alcohol while taking sleeping pills that contain barbiturates. These drugs, whose names usually end in -ital or -al like phenobarbital, do an effective job in depressing the central nervous system to help you sleep.

  Adding a few drinks to the sleeping pills can cause severe depression of the central nervous system, even death. When you hear about someone who "accidentally" overdosed, it may have been caused by barbiturates and alcohol.

- *Alcohol and aspirin*
  Aspirin itself can damage the stomach and cause discomfort. Some people can not take aspirin at all. Ingesting liquor and aspirin together can damage your stomach by causing irritation.

- *Alcohol and tranquilizers*
  Doctors prescribe tranquilizers to calm people down. The pills have a sedative effect. When they are combined with alcohol, an additive action takes place (remember 1 + 1 = 2?), and the effect is doubled. Your muscles are relaxed to the point of being impaired, and your judgment is clouded.

- *Alcohol and stimulants*
  Coffee, colas, tea, and other caffene-containing

drinks slow down the depressant effect of alcohol on the central nervous system but do not change the fact that when you drink alcohol your motor coordination and judgment are impaired.

Amphetamines such as the prescription drug Benzedrine and the illegal uppers or reds follow the same pattern.

• *Alcohol and insulin*
If you are diabetic, combining liquor with your insulin may cause your blood sugar level to drop faster than you would expect.

• *Alcohol and antihistamines*
Taking over-the-counter or prescription antihistamines for a cold, stuffy head and nose, or allergies and drinking has a synergistic effect (1 + 1 = 3, remember?). Your central nervous system is already depressed from the antihistamine, and you may get drowsy enough to endanger yourself and others if you use machinery or drive a car.

The above information is up-to-date, but as research continues and new drugs are put on the market (and new illegal drugs hit the street), other dangerous combinations of alcohol and drugs will be discovered. Although not everyone reacts as described above, there is ample reason for concern and caution.

Depend on your doctor and pharmacist to warn you of possible effects of mixing drugs, and stay away from the drug called alcohol if you are taking other drugs. Be aware of the dangers of double trouble.

CHAPTER 10

Drinking Problems

More than 100 million people drink alcohol in the United States. About 10 percent or maybe 10 million are alcoholics. Some of them are preteens and teenagers. How do these people, these kids, get to the point of being problem drinkers or to that final stage, alcoholics?

The difference between a problem drinker and an alcoholic is a fine line. It is difficult sometimes to tell the difference, since they have many characteristics in common.

Experts in the field of alcoholism agree that the following behavioral characteristics distinguish these drinkers from "social" drinkers.

• When faced with a stressful situation, abusers take a drink to "cope." When something shakes them up or they need some "courage," they reach for alcohol. You see it on TV all the time. Mr. X has a big decision to make. The phone looms threateningly on his desk; he must make that all-important call to his client. Quick! Rush to the bar, pour a shot of whiskey, and gulp it down. There now, Mr. X is all ready to go ahead with his business.

- Problem drinkers may not drink regularly, but when they do drink, it's not just one or two glasses of wine. It's whole bottles or two six-packs—whatever it takes to get completely bombed.
- Drinking first thing in the morning to "face the day" is a sign of a problem drinker. Even if the person is not physically addicted to alcohol, there is a psychological addiction. Showing up at school or work with alcohol on your breath and a few drinks under your belt means that you have a drinking problem.
- Drinkers who take risks when under the influence cause problems not only to themselves but to many innocent people. Driving a car, piloting a plane, operating machinery, participating in sports while drunk means that you are not taking into consideration what you risk for yourself and others. You are dangerous and you don't want to know it.
- People who hide bottles at home, in the car, in the school locker, in the garage, under the bush by the bus stop—all these are problem drinkers. They can't face the day without knowing that their supply is where they can get their hands on it when they need it. Hidden bottles equal security for these abusers.
- People who have blackouts have a drinking problem. If you can't remember where you went, what you did, how much you drank; if you "lose" a few hours or come to without being able to fill in the blanks in your mind, you are no longer a social drinker. You are out of control. Harrowing stories are told by former alcohol abusers, such as flying an

airplane from one city to another, being responsible
for 200 people, and not remembering a thing about
what happened on the flight.
- If your drinking is outside of society's "acceptable"
limits, you have a problem. If you drink when you
baby-sit or everytime you go on a trip with your
ski club, you have a problem. If you start drinking young, people will notice that you have a
problem.

The drinkers who become alcoholics have lost control
over their drinking and have a physical dependency or
addiction to alcohol.

Theories abound about why people become alcoholics.
Some experts feel that the illness builds up over a number
of years. Others believe that an abnormal physiological
reaction in the body causes them to become addicted to
alcohol while others do not.

Still others maintain that genetics has something to do
with a predisposition to alcoholism. That means that if
your parent or grandparent was an alcoholic, a family connection in your genes may bring about the disease.

Still others point out that people who do not have strong
coping skills seek to escape their problems through drinking and then become psychologically and emotionally
addicted to alcohol.

Although there is no concrete proof that any one of these
theories is correct, the fact remains that 10 percent of
drinkers *are* alcoholics. In other research it has been found
that teens and preteens take a shorter time to become
alcoholics than people who start drinking as adults.

Some of the signs of alcoholism, as described by Stanley
Englebardt in his book, *Kids and Alcohol, the Deadliest
Drug*, are the "morning-after miseries." When anyone

has too much to drink, the hangover the next morning is an uncomfortable reminder of overindulging.

The alcoholic's hangover is more painful, however, encompassing severe symptoms of uncontrollable shaking, excessive nausea and vomiting, abnormal sweating, and feelings of anxiety. In other words, you are sick. These are all results of your body's being addicted to or dependent on the drug alcohol and needing more. So you drink again to cover over those symptoms for a while longer.

Jasmine found a way to hide her symptoms from her father, with whom she lived during high school.

"My father got up earlier than I did for work. He always came in to make sure I was awake before he left. I'd sit bolt upright in bed the second he would wake me up. Then as soon as I heard him close the front door, I'd run for the bathroom and throw up before I went to school."

Jasmine's younger sister was frightened but kept her mouth shut because of Jasmine's threats. But when she found Jasmine passed out on the bathroom floor after vomiting blood, she called their dad at work. Jasmine's secret was finally out.

Another of the devastating symptoms of alcoholism is "DTs." When the alcoholic goes without alcohol for a period of time, the body runs out of the supply to which it is addicted. Delirium tremens, or DTs, takes over in the form of fever, unquenchable thirst, and hallucinations of horrible things happening to the body. One former alcoholic describes her DTs as "bugs moving all over my skin, inside and out, and I couldn't get them off no matter how hard I tried. I thought I was going crazy."

While you are dependent on alcohol, you pay little attention to nutrition and eating healthful foods. Malnutrition and internal disease shorten the alcoholic's life span by as much as ten to fifteen years.

Once you are an alcoholic, once your drinking habits are out of control and alcohol controls you, there is no cure. You either eventually die from the disease, or if you get help you can never drink again.

CHAPTER 11

The Four Stages

R ecent years have seen a slight decrease in some chemical abuse, but also a slight increase in the use of the drug alcohol. It used to be that teens drank alcohol or got high on other chemicals to prove that they were grown-up. It seemed the "adult" thing to do, like smoking cigarettes. By drinking and smoking, kids were assuming the role of adults.

Today it seems that alcohol, because it is the easiest drug to get, is being used by thousands of adolescents to block out the troubles they perceive in their lives. To cope with the stress and pressures of everyday living, teens and pre-teens drink in an effort to get rid of the frustrations and conflicts they meet daily.

"Going out and drinking on weekends," said Kara, fifteen, "is a way to blank out the week. If I flunked a test, had a fight with my stepmother, and broke my favorite necklace, by Friday I'm ready to scream. So I go out and get wasted, and by Sunday the pressure's off. I'm not an alcoholic. It just helps blow off my problems."

Maybe Kara will be lucky. Not all young drinkers be-come alcoholics. Not even those who drink somewhat heavily become addicted. Kids go through stages to reach the alcoholic level. It can take up to seven years for an adult to reach the alcoholic stage, but kids can bottom out in one to two years.

Stage 1

Joey was nine. He snuck a beer from his house for the first time and brought it over to Pete's garage. There, hiding under the staircase, they shared their first beer and felt a little "high."

Stage 1 is the beginning phase of alcohol use. It involves experimental use or sneaking a drink at a social event. Usually on weekends or in the summer, grade school and junior high kids try out what they've been hearing and seeing—that drinking is okay. It's fun. It's sexy. It's great!

Drinking at this phase is usually done with friends, and the attraction is to see what it's all about. There's a bit of a thrill in acting "grown-up" and excitement in doing something "forbidden".

Tolerance is low, and it's easy to feel a buzz because the body has never had to contend with this substance before. Defying parents and adults is part of the high. Kids expect to feel great and have fun, and so that becomes true for this experimentation time.

Lynn and her friends wanted to do something "fun" for their junior high Christmas dance. "I stole some scotch from my father's bottle at home and took it to Patty's house for a sleep-over. We were getting ready for the dance, and I whipped out this jar full of scotch. We wanted to have a good time at the dance, and we figured that if we got a little drunk, we could."

Since it was the first time for Lynn and her friends, the

bitter taste of the scotch put an end to the thought of finishing off the jar.

"Ugh, it was awful tasting!" Lynn said. "But we still wanted to do something exciting. So we wet our lips with the scotch a few times so the other kids could smell it on our breath. Patty even used it like perfume. You know, like dabbing some on her wrists and throat. Then we acted drunk and all the kids thought we were. It was cool!"

Being cool and doing things that older teens do is an attraction for younger kids. Wanting to do what a seventeen-year-old brother does is on many a kid's wish list. Being in a hurry to grow up and get out of the awkward preteens is a problem that hassles a lot of kids.

There are many other ways to cope with that inner need to be grown-up and do the things you see on TV and videos. Going out and drinking may not be the wisest choice, especially if you are not aware of the risks you are taking. Every alcoholic teenager in a drug rehabilitation hospital was a beginner at one time.

How do you know that you will stay at this stage and never progress to the next? Are you strong enough in your self-esteem to keep yourself from using alcohol as an escape from problems? Are eight-, ten-, or twelve-year-olds ready for the physical, mental, and emotional consequences of using and abusing alcohol?

There are always choices. You have the choice to start drinking, to stop drinking, and never to begin. Read on to the next stages that kids have traveled. All those kids started right here at Stage 1:

- Uses alcohol to relieve tension.
- Once started, seeks more opportunities to drink.
- Moves with a drinking crowd.
- Starts building up a tolerance to alcohol.

Stage 2

Using more, drinking more, does not always by itself indicate dependency, but a regular pattern of use can be a move toward addiction.

The main point to remember at Stage 2 is not so much how much or how often alcohol is used, but *why* this drug is being used. Behavioral changes accompany Stage 2 as a result of regular use of alcohol. Adolescents in this phase of their drinking habit may lie about why their allowance goes so fast. Their grades may go down, or they may start dropping out of sports and activities that they previously enjoyed.

"Well, I used to drink only about once a month with my friends," said thirteen-year-old Adam. "Then I really got to liking vodka because I could hardly taste it when I mixed it with juice or soda. We'd get a bottle from Kirk's older brother every once in a while and only drink half of it at a time. But then we started doing it more and more."

A cycle begins. You start lying to your parents and family about your allowance or savings account being gone, or about being at Joe's house when you really were at Jack's house (whom you're forbidden to see). You start feeling guilty about the lies, and you get caught in a web of more lying to cover the first lies. You may get angry at yourself and not see a way out of this cycle.

So you drink more often to get rid of the guilt and self-hate. You keep disappointing your parents, and that makes you feel ashamed. So you drink still more often to blot it out. Once this cycle begins, you are at risk for dependency/addiction.

Patterns of alcohol use and abuse in Stage 2 include increased tolerance (your body seems to be able to "handle" more alcohol) and more use of whole cases of beer or entire bottles of wine or hard liquor. Sometimes drinking "sophisticated" beers or name-brand wines becomes important, and you look down on store brands.

Adolescents in this stage believe that they can "handle" their drinking and may feel proud when they finish off larger amounts of alcohol. Using and abusing becomes more frequent. No longer do they wait for a holiday, a vacation, or even the weekend. Weeknights seem to be just as good a time to drink.

"I really didn't think I was having a problem with alcohol at that time," said MaryBeth, fourteen. "My friends and I just started getting into it more, you know? Almost like we didn't realize it. I mean, we'd even spike our thermos bottles for lunch. I remember lying to my mother about why I was taking a thermos to school after three years of refusing to be seen with one. She believed me, though. It was easy."

Kids in Stage 2 are becoming preoccupied with drinking. They carefully plan and anticipate their next high. They may worry about their source of supply. Will Gena's older sister's boyfriend come through with that bottle of rum for Friday? They may start having a hard time "making it through" the days to the next opportunity to get high, and worrying about it. Experimentation with other drugs can enter the scene here.

More money is spent as alcohol is bought rather than snitched from home. Risk-taking enters the picture, and they do things they may not have done before, such as stealing expensive wine from the house where they baby-sit.

Stage 2 kids think they are functioning normally when they are high, and they concentrate on fooling others.

Nondrinking friends are dropped, and more time is spent with drinking friends, who often are not introduced to parents.

It's about this time that they start getting "caught" by parents and at school. They are punished for cutting classes, get detention for coming to school late, are suspended for telling off a teacher. They are grounded for breaking curfew or sneaking out when told to stay home.

In many cases, Stage 2 kids are punished for inappropriate behavior and not for the growing dependence on alcohol. Fooling everyone into thinking there's no problem is important at this stage.

Do you see yourself fitting into these patterns? Have you ventured beyond that Stage 1 experimentation/social use and moved into this darker world of regular use? Are you trapped in the cycle of use guilt remorse more use? Once on this merry-go-round, you are at high risk for moving on to Stage 3.

Some kids in this age group, maybe junior high to early senior high school, use alcohol in a social/regular pattern but do not become dependent. A few use alcohol with little side effect and still function on a normal level. These are the "heavy drinkers" who have not crossed over the invisible line into addiction/dependency, the next stage on the road to alcoholism.

There is no clear-cut way to see it happen. It may be gradual or it may be quick, but it does happen to a lot of kids. Many do cross over that line from Stage 2:

• Want alcohol more.
• Must drink larger amounts of alcohol than before.
• Seek to get drunk more often.
• Drink sneakily.

- Feel guilty.
- May forget or "black out" what happens when drinking.

Stage 3

In this stage teens begin to use alcohol regularly. They spend more and more time, energy, and money thinking about and planning on getting high. The frequency of getting high every week increases, sometimes to every day.

Daily preoccupation with being high becomes a "normal" life-style for a Stage 3 drinker. Very few of his or her daily activities do not revolve around alcohol.

Dave has a job after school stocking shelves at a food store. He has been warned about his careless mistakes in pricing the items. What his boss doesn't know is that Dave drinks every afternoon before he comes to work. He says it "helps him pass the time."

The social drinking urge is being replaced. Getting high is no longer enough; being "wasted" or "blasted" is the goal. Often Leslie drinks by herself, in isolation. She doesn't share her stuff with her friends anymore because she's afraid there won't be enough, and having a sure supply is of utmost importance.

At this stage, Fred is looking for a "better" high, so he tries mixing alcohol with other drugs. The high he gets from drinking isn't enough to satisfy him, so the risk of combining drugs doesn't mean much. Getting as high as he can is the only goal. Fred also starts dealing drugs because he needs money to support his own habit. Kids needing money at this point steal things from home—TVs, VCRs, radios, and the like—to get a fast return.

Schoolwork and attendance are affected. Stage 3 kids miss Monday mornings a lot because they haven't recovered from their weekend binge. Pam gets back late from lunch most days because she had to duck home for a few drinks. She doesn't even make it to her last two classes on Fridays. That's when she starts her weekend routine of taking money to her boyfriend's sister, who buys them their three-day supply of booze. What else is a weekend for, anyway?

"I was sure this kid was drinking," said Joe Brown, a substance abuse counselor, "but there was nothing I could do to convince the parents. They had never seen Kevin high and thought that the changes in his behavior such as failing grades were normal adolescent stuff."

Joe finally persuaded Kevin's parents to let him come over to talk to them in Kevin's presence.

"This kid was so great at fooling everyone that I finally said to his parents, 'I bet if we searched his room right now, we'd find some bottles.' His mother assured me that we wouldn't, that his room was always immaculate and he always cleaned it himself."

Joe knew then he was on to something. Drinking kids whose parents never had to clean their room were hiding something. Joe's experience told him he was on the right track.

Kevin led them to the neatest, cleanest teenager's room that Joe had ever seen. It was spotless, organized, so tidy that not even a piece of paper was out of place. Kevin watched with an innocent look on his face as Joe opened drawers and searched closets and boxes to no avail.

Then Joe looked at Kevin's bed. It was perfectly made, as if ready for an Army inspection. When he commented on it, Kevin's mother proudly said that Kevin never let her touch his bed. He changed the sheets himself and she didn't even have to smooth out a wrinkle.

In one swipe, Joe yanked the covers off Kevin's bed and lifted the mattress. There, lying neatly side by side, were fourteen empty vodka bottles.

Hiding bottles is another sympton of a Stage 3 user. Lying and hiding bad report cards and school discipline letters from parents become the norm. Teachers notice him or her sleeping through classes and "forgetting" to hand in assignments. School becomes secondary to drinking and the next "high."

Kids start getting into legal hassles around this time, driving around with older kids. Monica's mother got that dreaded phone call on Friday night. "This is the Middletown Police Department. We have your daughter here at the station house."

"Is she all right? Is she hurt?" Monica's mom holds her breath as most parents do.

"There's been no accident, but she is being arrested for underage consumption and illegal buying of alcoholic beverages."

Beginning a police record as a juvenile offender is not as impossible as some kids think. Using fake identification saying you're twenty-one when you are really seventeen is illegal, and you can be arrested for it. Driving around drinking a six-pack of beer is against the law.

"We weren't hurting anyone," Larry protested. "All we had were a few drinks, and the cops pulled us over for a taillight they said was out. Yeah, right. They just wanted to get us for something. It must have been a slow night and they were looking for kids to get in trouble."

What Larry "got" was arrested for DWI (Driving While Intoxicated); because he was eighteen years old, he spent the night in jail, had to pay a hefty fine, lost his license and driving privilege for 60 days, and had to do time in community service. He now had a police record and was put on probation. His insurance company added a $700 surcharge on his policy because he was now a "risk."

In personal habits Stage 3 users change. In males, grooming habits suffer. Jerry, who at age eight couldn't wait until the day he shaved, now perpetually has a few days worth of scraggly beard on his chin. He forgets to change clothes, wearing the same jeans and T-shirt for several days. Morning showers fall by the wayside, as personal hygiene is no longer important.

On the other hand, females in this phase may tend to get neater. They try to cover up their drinking and work hard to appear normal. Special care is devoted to hair, makeup, and clothes so that parents won't have anything for which to criticize them.

During Stage 3 some kids become worried. In sober moments they realize how alcohol has changed their lives, their friends, their school record, and their relationship with their family. They may think about quitting.

Karen, fourteen, was finally convinced after blacking out and not remembering what she had done for three whole hours. Maybe she needed to cut down or quit because things were getting out of hand. Anyway she was grounded by her parents for poor grades and driving in her boyfriend's car without permission.

"For the next three weeks I'm not going to drink at all. I'll keep my parents happy and show them that I am not an alcoholic as they think I am."

Karen did it. She didn't touch a drop for three weeks. She didn't feel very well, and her hands shook every morning, but she was determined to do it. Her parents were pleased that Karen seemed to have kicked her drinking habit, and Karen herself was proud to have stayed sober all that time. It was the longest she had ever gone in the two years she had been drinking.

See, no problem, right? Karen can stop drinking and stay sober for *all that time*, so she really isn't a Stage 3 drinker, is she?

After proving to herself that she could do it, Karen celebrated by getting drunk the next weekend. But now she had a false sense of security that she could stop whenever she wanted. She felt that she had a choice whether to drink or not. Unfortunately, for Stage 3 abusers the choice is always the same: to keep on drinking.

Family relationships really deteriorate at this point. Because the teen's personality undergoes some very obvious changes at this level of alcohol abuse, fights and open warfare with parents and siblings are bound to happen. The teenager feels that the parents want to keep him or her from having "fun" or from growing up and making decisions. Behavior changes, and the family has a hard time recognizing the teen who used to live with them. He or she becomes a stranger to them, sometimes an unwanted stranger.

"The hardest thing I had to do was the 'tough love' bit," Rich's mother said. "I guess I had been covering up for his drinking and enabled him to keep right on doing it and get worse. Then when I tried to get him to stop, I found I had little control over my son. It was scary."

Because Rich would threaten and physically hurt his younger brother when he came home drunk, his mother decided that the only control she had was to protect her younger son. She had the locks on the doors changed and heavy-duty bolts put on the windows. On the nights when she knew that Rich would come home drunk, aggressive, and out of control, she locked him out of the house.

"It was as if we were in prison. Rich would pound on the

doors and curse us out. It was frightening and hard to believe that this maniac screaming filthy names at me used to crawl into my lap for a good-night kiss."

Kids who are bogged down in Stage 3 alcohol abuse may end up in a hospital after a severe drinking bout. Once you have reached this level, you need to be in counseling with a certified alcoholism counselor. Through your school or hospital, you and your family can get help to put you back on the road to sobriety and help you stay there. Sometime during this stage, you may realize that this is not the way you want to continue your life, and you may seek help. It is out there. You have to want it.

Stage 3:

- Has many rational reasons for drinking.
- Is out of control once drinking starts.
- Blacks out more often.
- Has reputation of being a drinker.
- Displays aggressive behavior on binges.
- Considers family and friends no longer important.
- Drinks in the morning.
- Is irresponsible and careless.
- May be hospitalized.

Stage 4

If an adolescent has not accepted help by now, chances are that he or she will reach this stage of addiction. For teens and preteens in Stage 4 being high all the time is "normal." This delusion is maintained against any argument a parent or other person may present. No matter how overwhelming the evidence that their alcohol use is out of control, abusers maintain that there is no problem. Even presented with evidence that alcohol is socially, emotionally, and physically killing them, "I'm fine. I can handle it," is the usual response.

Daily preoccupation with drinking and being high is the pattern in Stage 4. Most of the teen's time, energy, and money go into getting high and making sure that there is no break in the alcohol supply.

Peter, now addicted, drinks before school, at lunchtime, after school, at work, and on weekends. He needs alcohol to cope and has probably turned to harder drugs, possibly injecting them.

Cathy, now completely dependent on alcohol, has more frequent illnesses. Minor bruises appear more readily on her skin because the capillaries are extended toward the outer layer of skin with the overuse of alcohol. She is colder now, too, and wears layers of clothes to keep warm.

Bryan, sixteen, a Stage 4 alcoholic, finds that his normal life-style includes problems with school, his parents, the police, his employer, his probation officer, and his friends. He has lost control over his use of alcohol and drinks to intoxication most of the time. His blackouts become more frequent.

Tammy, fifteen, experiences torment when she is sober and quickly drinks herself back to the "feeling-no-pain" stage. If you ask Tammy what she did all day, just about every activity she mentions will be connected with her alcohol use.

Danny feels that his family is out to get him. "My friends are the only ones who stick with me," Danny says, and he's proud to be a burnout like his buddies. His family have given up on him and kicked him out of the house. They have changed the locks on the doors, and they call the police when they find him sleeping on the back porch.

Malnutrition afflicts many Stage 4 kids. Since drinking is the only important "food" to them, nutrition goes out the window. Fruits? Vegetables? Are you kidding? Be real. When she's not drinking, Donna grabs a burger at a fast-food place, but she usually saves her money to pay her supplier.

At this stage there is a lot of self-hate. Alcoholic kids try to drink away the guilt feelings. Self-esteem goes under, and they feel loss of control. They can't *not* drink. Thoughts of suicide and actual attempts occur. The old alibi system for drinking gives way, and it is at this point that abusers may reaches the point where they figure they had better get help or they'll die.

These teens need to be involved in a licensed treatment program, a "rehab," or in serious treatment with a certified alcoholism/substance abuse counselor as quickly as possible.

If you recognize yourself or one of your friends at Stage 4, you may believe there is no help, or you may still deny that you have a problem. Probably you are not thinking very clearly, but you've reached a turning point in your life. Reach out and tell someone that you don't want to die, that you want to live and that you need help before it is too late.

Your school counselor or in-house substance abuse counselor, your doctor, a hotline, or an emergency program can get you help. It's a difficult road to recovery and sobriety, but if the only other choice is to die, then take that first step! Say "I need help," and many people will be there to help you.

Stage 4:

• Has no more control over alcohol use.
• Drinks every day, all the time.
• Never stops drinking until drunk.

- May drink for days at a time, remembering little or nothing.
- When sober, feels sick and tormented, shaky.
- Drinks any kind of alcohol.
- Can't even give reasons for drinking anymore; just has to do it.
- Must get help or face the real possibility of dying.

CHAPTER 12

Brian's Story

"**B**eing the youngest of four boys, I never got very much attention. My parents both worked, and it was usually up to one of my older brothers to keep an eye on me. They were never thrilled to have me tagging along, and most of the time I felt I was in the way.

"This one night my parents were going out with friends. They went out a lot too and usually came home drunk. I was eleven at the time, and since my brothers were told not to leave me alone, Mark and Bobby took me with them to a party.

"My idea of a party was still the birthday kind—you know, cake and ice cream or a sleep-over where you stayed up late and ate and watched TV. This was sure a different kind of party.

"The drinks were all over the house. All I had to do was pick up a half-empty glass and finish it. I didn't like the taste too much, but after five or six drinks I got kinda high. I was having a hard time talking and walking, and all the older kids thought it was really funny.

"That night I got a lot of attention. Everyone wanted to see the kid who was drunk. I tried to tell jokes, and everyone laughed at them. I felt great! I was the hit of the party. Even my brothers thought I was cool and gave me some cigarettes to smoke. I had tried them before too, but now I thought I looked so cool and grown-up, like these older kids.

"Finally I was getting attention. I was having fun. Drinking and getting high was fun. I wanted to do it more.

"The next weekend I asked Mark if I could go with them again. They weren't real glad to do it, but Mom and Dad were going out again, and one of them would have had to stay home with me. So I went to another party. And I drank all I could. And I was funny and people laughed at my jokes and how I staggered around.

"On the way home, though, I threw up all over the back seat of Mark's car, and they were really mad. They had to clean the car when we got home, and all I could do was lie on the grass and laugh.

"Mom kinda guessed what had happened, but she didn't come right out and ask me if I was drinking or anything, so I figured I was safe.

"All that week I kept thinking about going out again and getting drunk with my brothers. I never did really well in school, and now I didn't care. I thought about the weekend and drinking and that's all.

"But before Friday night came, my parents had a big fight about Dad's staying out late without Mom. It was okay if she went out drinking with him, but if he went out by himself she'd scream and yell, and he'd pack up and leave for a few days to punish her or something. Then she'd stay home and drink and cry about how bad she had it and he was no good and stuff like that. This was about the sixth or seventh time he'd done it.

"So instead of going out with Mark and Bobby (I think they were glad), I had to stay home and listen to Mom. My oldest brother, Steve, hardly ever was home, so when she complained and cried, she'd blame Dad and me for all her problems.

"I was fed up with her complaints about no one listening to her or doing anything for her, and how rotten I was. So after she had drunk half the scotch in the bottle, I finished off the rest. She was too drunk to care, and I was too miserable to care if she cared.

"That started a new pattern in my life. Every weekend I either went out with my brothers and got drunk or stayed home with my mother and got drunk after she got drunk. My father never came back after that last time, so I was really on my own because none of my brothers listened to my mother.

"I learned how to fake a lot of things, like keeping my grades up to the C-D level so I didn't get kicked out of school or my teacher wouldn't call my mother. As long as I didn't cause any problems, no one bothered me much. It was almost as if I was invisible, and only when I got drunk and partied with my brothers and their friends did I feel important. So that's what I did to keep feeling important. I drank on weekends for almost two years.

"One day Mom got divorce papers in the mail. She went off the wall, drank a whole lot, and took off with the car. Mark and Bobby were mad because they didn't have a car to use that night. Me, I was kinda worried about Mom. She never came home that night.

"We got a call from the hospital the next morning. She was pretty badly hurt in a car accident. A one-car accident. I figured that either she was too drunk to drive or she had tried to kill herself. That really scared me. My brothers were pretty much on their own, and Dad was gone for good. She was all I had left. If she died, what would I do?

"When I went to see Mom in the hospital, she was drugged up for the pain. At least she was alive. About a week later when I visited her, there was a woman in her room talking to her. Mom told me to stay, that I needed to hear what this woman had to say too. At first I couldn't figure out what she *was* saying.

"She was telling Mom how lonely and empty she had felt when her husband had left her and that she had started drinking to get rid of her pain. The court had taken her kids away because she wasn't taking care of them right.

"I looked at Mom, and she was crying. She said, 'If they ever took Brian away from me, I'd really die.' That got me scared. Here I had been thinking how great it was to drink with my brothers and even with my mother. I never thought that I'd be taken away and lose my whole family. I got chills thinking about it.

"Then this woman said that she had sobered up by going to Alcoholics Anonymous meetings and getting counseling. She's been sober for four years, and her kids are doing good too because they go to Alateen meetings. Alateen is for kids whose parent drinks.

"Mom turned to me and said, 'Brian, I'm so sorry for all of this. I'm really sick with all the drinking, and I'm an alcoholic. I'm going to get help. And so are you.'

"I wish I could say that everyone lived happily ever after, but we didn't. The more I thought about it, the more I knew my brothers were alcoholics too, and so was I. We all needed help.

"We didn't all want help. I figured that if Mom was getting help, I could still drink sometimes; I wasn't going to be taken away or anything. Then one night I blacked out. I mean I really blacked out and didn't remember anything until I woke up the next day with my hand all cut up.

From what I was told, I got crazy and smashed my hand through a window at a kid's house.

"All the dried blood scared me. When my mother saw it, she just said, 'Bri, it's time you got help too.' I think I knew then that I had to.

"I started going to AA meetings when I was fourteen. For the first few months AA didn't make much sense to me. I'd catch on and then slip up. It took me more than a year to stay sober for five months straight. That's where I am right now. Five months sober and taking it one day at a time.

"I think what helped me was that I started talking about me and my sickness, and I found that no one hated me for it. I talked to other kids who were where I had been two years ago, and ya know what? Some of them really listened to me. One kid, a twelve-year-old, came up to me after one talk at a teen AA meeting and asked if he could call me to talk if he felt like taking a drink, and I said yes. I felt really good to help someone else.

"My Mom and I are sober. I wish I could say the same for Mark and Bobby, but they have to reach their own point to *want* to stop drinking. I can't do it for them.

"I still go to parties, and kids try to get me to drink. It's real hard not to, and sometimes I swear I'll never go to another one. I'm afraid. I know that if I even take one sip I'm gone, back to where I was. I know that I have a disease that can't be cured. But I control it and not let it control me.

"There's lots of kids out there like me. I got help finally. If you're like me, I hope you do too."

CHAPTER 13

Student Assistance Programs

With more teens drinking and more teens becoming problem drinkers, it follows that there are more teenage alcoholics. High schools around the country are creating programs to prevent alcohol problems among their students while intervening with those already hooked.

For a long time high schools and middle schools did piecemeal work in trying to prevent alcohol and drug abuse. In recent years, however, there has been a concentrated and coordinated effort to work with kids who are abusing.

"Every school shapes its program differently," says certified substance abuse counselor Vickie Wilson. "What we provide in our high school is short-term intervention counseling. We assess the student's needs and the family's needs. Sometimes the family's needs color what the student really needs to work on and get help for."

A lot of kids come in to discuss their family problems at

the Student Assistance Program (SAP) office. Often, after an initial session or two, a connection to alcohol and drugs is uncovered. Many emotional problems are interconnected with abuse of alcohol and other drugs.

"My friend kinda twisted my arm to go see our SAP counselor," said Marie, a freshman. "I had tried to cover up some bruises on my arms, but my friend said I should stop hiding what was happening to me. At first I was uncomfortable talking to a stranger. But the counselor really helped."

Marie was finally able to tell someone about her abusive alcoholic father. She needed to feel that she could trust someone without it backfiring on her. By attending Alateen meetings and taking her nondrinking mother to Al-Anon, Marie was able to work out a better understanding of her life and deal with her father in a way that was not harmful to her. Her SAP counselor kept up a supportive relationship in school while the AA-affliated programs helped her on the outside.

"Kids are referred to us through varied avenues," Wilson said. "Sometimes they have just had enough in their life and have heard that SAP can help them. Others bring in their friends, as Marie's friend did. Sometimes parents call us and want us to assess their child without the kid's knowing that the parent made the contact."

Teens and preteens caught high in school arrive at SAP via the discipline route. These kids are required to see a counselor within the school setting as part of their treatment program. Often teachers, school nurses, counselors, and administrators ask an SAP counselor to see a kid they suspect has an alcohol or drug problem.

However an abusing student ends up at SAP, help is immediately available.

"Once the problem is uncovered," Wilson continued,

"convincing the student that he or she needs help is the next step. There's a lot of counseling and talking to the student about what help is available and how to take that first step toward recovering from an abusing life-style."

Sometimes short-term contracts are worked out. Not drinking for the weekend or for three consecutive days is the initial goal. The student returns to talk about how he or she felt about and coped with not drinking. Then the contract is extended, supported by SAP counseling and contacts.

"The hard-core abusing kids try to avoid us," Wilson said. "They aren't ready to admit they need help or have a problem. Those are the kids who most likely need a rehabilitation program. But we can't rehabilitate someone who doesn't want it."

For the kids who need a rehab and agree to go, the SAP counselor makes arrangements with an inpatient or out-patient facility and walks the parent through the initial steps and interview procedure, thereby helping the entire family on the way to getting help for the abusing student.

"I finally had had it," said Jim, fourteen. "I was bad off, drinking in the morning, bringing stuff to school, falling asleep in all my classes. I had already bombed out of one rehab, but my counselor at school never gave up on me. When I was ready, really ready, for rehab she got me in."

At the facility, the student is interviewed and evaluated, and contact is made with the SAP counselor. The family ultimately decides on the placement for their child.

"In the past we've had to scramble to get a bed for a kid. But lately we've been able to place abusing students in a program. More spaces are available, and more facilities are opening up for kids now," Wilson said.

"Insurance can be a determining factor in whether or not the student gets a bed in a rehab," she added. "If the family has no insurance to cover the expenses, the family may have to go on a waiting list or seek other alternatives."

After rehab the student usually goes to an aftercare program. When he or she returns to the home school after weeks or months, the SAP counselor picks up the in-school counseling, offering a home base to kids who are shaky and apprehensive about reentering the place where some of their problems were known.

Rehabilitation referrals are only a small part of a Student Assistance Program. Many programs around the country offer multiple components, including:

- Counseling or treatment for alcohol and drug abusing students;
- Supportive education and group counseling sessions for students with alcoholic parents;
- Preventive sessions for at-risk kids who are performing poorly in school and are potential dropouts;
- Parenting classes;
- Teacher inservice and prevention training programs;
- Class presentations about alcohol and drug abuse;
- Training of school staff members on substance abuse or areas that are symptomatic of substance abuse, such as suicide or depression;
- Schoolwide, communitywide, and statewide programs for drunk driving awareness at prom and graduation times.

"A main point we want to get across to all the kids is that help is available. A lot of kids don't see drinking as a problem. They see it as socially acceptable and not in the category of hard drugs," Wilson said. "Athletes especially perceive drugs as bad but will go out and polish off a case of beer as a victory celebration every Saturday night and still not think that they have a problem."

The most important aspect of a Student Assistance Program anywhere across the nation is that kids feel free to come in when they have a problem. If kids have a safe place where they can start to get help for drinking and whatever else is going wrong in their lives without fear of reprisal or stigma, they will take that first step. When kids feel that things are out of control and they feel the need to abuse, it's necessary for them to know that they have alternatives and choices, rather than turning to that bottle they have hidden in their closet.

CHAPTER ◇ 14

Counseling

"I knew I needed help with my drinking, but I didn't know where to get it."

"My parents told me I was going for help and that was it."

"My father said he wouldn't pay for counseling, so I spent a lot of time with a youth adviser from my friend's church."

"I refused to go for counseling at first. Figured I didn't need help, but my girlfriend said that either I get help or we're through."

However you come to realize that you need help with your alcohol habits, seeing a counselor who has experience working with kids your age can put you on track. Some kids decide on their own. Others have to be strongly encouraged because they aren't sure about themselves, whether they need help, whether they have a drinking problem, or why they should go.

If you have had problems with your family, teachers, school, neighbors, friends, or the police because of your drinking, alcohol is interfering with your life. If you like to drink but feel guilty and upset about the consequences you suffer after the drinking's over, maybe you are ready for counseling.

Or maybe you agree to go for help only because your parents will kick you out or your boyfriend will break up with you if you don't.

Kids arrive at counselor's offices all different ways. Something prompts you to get there. Use the opportunity to make some positive, healthful moves in your life.

"I was so scared when my mom made the appointment with Mrs. P.," fourteen-year-old Danny said. "I didn't know what I was supposed to say, so I just kept my mouth shut.

"Mrs. P. didn't come on real strong. She asked me a few questions, and then we sat with no one talking. I couldn't take much of that, so I started telling her about school. That was the first time. It wasn't horrible or anything, but it made it easier to go back. I finally did tell her about my drinking about the third session. She helped me clear up a few things about myself and my friends. I've stayed away from drinking for a while now."

Going for professional help still carries some myths around it. You don't have to be "crazy" to see a psychiatrist or a family counselor. You don't have to post it on the school bulletin board either. No one needs to know.

Depending on your own needs, your family's finances, and your parents' cooperation, you can find a counselor who is right to help you with your alcohol abuse. You might see a psychologist or a social worker in private practice, a family counselor either in a clinic or private office, or a youth counselor or clergyperson from your church or synagogue.

There are many alcoholism and substance abuse counselors, usually licensed and with special training to help you with your drinking. If you are not sure where to go, talk to your school guidance counselor or substance abuse counselor, who can provide names and phone numbers of agencies or therapists where you can get help.

You might be referred to a family counseling agency or a mental health clinic. These places have trained counselors who can help you deal with your reasons for drinking and your alcohol habits. The counselors have various qualifications and college degrees, and you'll be able to find someone who is skilled and empathetic to help you cope.

A psychiatrist is a medical doctor (MD), a physician who has extensive training in helping people with psychological and emotional problems. You may decide to work with someone like this because you have underlying problems that you feel are a cause of your alcohol abuse.

Perhaps you and your family choose to get counseling from a psychologist. Psychologists have college degrees, always a master's degree and usually a PhD, which is a doctorate, the highest degree you can get in college. Their study centered on clinical psychology, which means that they spent time in the field training and working with people with emotional problems.

Therapists who are social workers have a college degree called Master of Social Work (MSW). These counselors work with the emotional and physical aspects of social problems. Many of them have experience and training in psychiatric social work.

Family counselors may be licensed by the state and have master's degrees in psychology and marriage/family counseling. Not every state has licensing qualifications, so watch out for someone who just hangs up a sign but is not qualified to work with the problems in your life.

In youth centers counselors may not have college degrees but may have experienced some of the same problems you have and can offer warm feelings and good listening skills. Your priest, rabbi, or minister also has experience in working with people who have problems in their lives.

No matter what the diplomas say, you need to find a counselor whom you can trust and depend on to work with you in a helpful, constructive way. If your counselor starts right in at the first session harping on the things you've done wrong, look for another counselor.

Ideally your counselor should help you find ways of dealing with your drinking and any underlying problems that alcohol may be covering up. Getting your parents involved can help. Your parents may not know how to deal with you and your drinking, so family counseling can help them too.

Another way to get help is through group sessions. Other kids are struggling with similar problems. Some of them may have ideas on how to lick those problems. Others will share their feelings of helplessness or hopelessness, and you'll find that you are not alone. Finding out what has worked and what hasn't can give you ideas on working with your alcohol abuse. It can also be a way to make new friends upon whom you can lean and gather strength as you cope with your drinking.

If you are afraid to go right into that professional field, start with a hotline. Trained people answer the phones. They will listen to you and refer you to an appropriate place to get help. Sometimes an anonymous person who cares can start you on that first step toward getting help.

Counseling can cost nothing or can cost you and your

family thousands of dollars. Special centers like youth houses or crisis centers in organizations like the YMCA don't charge for their services. Your clergyperson will help at no charge. Your guidance counselor, school alcohol/ substance abuse counselor, social worker, or school psychologist can help, although they are not in a position to handle weekly therapy programs.

Sliding scales are used at clinics and mental health centers. You are charged according to your ability to pay and your family income. Your parent's health insurance may pay for the help you need.

Some places require parental permission to work with you. Others do not. Many times having your parents involved will make you stronger. Some parents resist. Maybe there are no parents to count on. Whatever the case, getting help before alcohol takes over your life is the most important point of counseling.

Counseling isn't magic. All your problems don't clear up after one session. You may need to explore some painful beliefs and situations in your life, and you must be willing to work on yourself to get the results you seek.

CHAPTER ◊ 15

Rehab

Rehabilitation programs for preteens and teens with
alcohol abuse problems take several forms. Most
kids attend either an outpatient or a residential
treatment program. Both can be followed by an aftercare
or extended-care program.

If kids are ready to seek a life of sobriety, they can take
part in a full-time program during the day but go home at
night. That is an outpatient rehab. Leslie attended one
near her home.

"I knew I needed help, but I needed some of that help
from my family, so my parents and I decided on a rehab
close by. I go five days a week from nine in the morning
until four in the afternoon. On Saturdays my parents and I
attend a morning family counseling group."

Typically in a daily rehab you start with exercise. The
mornings usually are times for education: films, videos,
and lectures where kids learn about addictive personali-
ties, facing reality, alcoholism progression, and other
pertinent topics.

The rest of the day is spent in group counseling and
therapy. "The group work is tough," Leslie says. "Most of

us at first don't want to admit how big our drinking problem is. Some kids say they're here because their parents
made them come. That may be true, but since they're
here, they might as well face truth."

Group counseling permits interaction that can break
down the barriers kids put up. Denial is a strong protection
and something that every alcoholic has to work through.
Addiction seems to be the only disease that tells people
that they don't have a problem. Kids go to great lengths to
convince themselves and others that there's "no problem."

Leslie's rehab lasted for four weeks. It was followed by
an aftercare program once a week for thirteen more weeks.
There she participated in more group therapy and counseling as well as an alcohol education program.

"We also had time in rehab to do school work. The clinic
provided tutors so that we didn't get too far behind in
our classes. It was hard enough going back to school after
being out for four weeks, but not being behind in my work
helped."

George needed a more intensive program. His family,
on the recommendation of their doctor, enrolled him in a
residential program. This was an intensive program in
group and individual therapy, films and lectures, opportunities to develop greater self-awareness, and knowledge
of his disease and of his relationships with other people.

Most residential and outpatient programs have in-house
meetings of Alcoholics Anonymous, Al-Anon, and Alateen.
Each participant is encouraged to use the support offered
by these programs and receives contacts to make when
leaving the rehab. Continued attendance at AA meetings
is a strong component in a rehabilitation and recovery/
sobriety program.

Therapy affords the patients a way to relearn com-
munication skills, to accept personal responsibility, and

to get in touch with feelings they may have blocked out for a long time. In group, George was able to get feedback from the staff and other kids.

"Especially when I tried to put something over on the other kids," he said with a rueful grin. "The kids who had been there longer could tell when I put on the bull, and they let me have it. 'Hey George, that's not how you really feel. You're saying you're glad to be recovering, but your face looks like a stone wall.' Stuff like that. I had to face things and put my real feelings out in the open. It was uncomfortable, but it helped in the long run."

Residential programs want the family involved from day one. Chemical dependency is a family problem, and usually the entire family needs treatment. Parents of teens especially need to be taught ways to deal with their own attitudes and emotions. There are family group sessions and individual and group educational meetings with the counselors involved in the teen's treatment.

"I was in rehab for three months. My parents drove an hour each way on Tuesday nights and Saturday mornings every week I was there," George said. "We all needed to straighten things out in our heads and get along better. The groups helped us face our problems, and I was able to see that I wasn't the absolute cause of our family breakdown, maybe more the result of it."

The professional staff at rehabs are highly skilled and throughly trained professionals including doctors, nurses, psychologists, family counselors, and state certified alcoholism and substance abuse counselors. They all work together to help the alcoholic adolescent face this serious, life-threatening illness and begin the long, difficult journey back to sobriety.

A typical day at a residential treatment program is illustrated in the accompanying chart.

Daily Activity Schedule

Time	Monday	Tuesday	Wednesday	Thursday	Friday	Saturday	Sunday
6:30	Wake Up	Wake Up	Wake Up	Wake Up	Wake up	Breakfast	Wake up
7:30	Breakfast	Breakfast	Breakfast	Breakfast	Breakfast	(optional)	Breakfast
8:15	Community	Exercise/	Exercise/	Exercise/	Exercise/		
8:45	Meeting	Aerobic	Aerobic	Aerobic	Aerobic		
9:00	Lecture	Lecture	Lecture	Lecture	Lecture	Community	Family Group
9:30						Meeting	Church (optional)
10:00	Group	Group	Group	Group	Group	Group	Lecture
10:30						Nutrition Lecture	
11:00	Job Function	Job Function	Job Function	Job Function	Job Function	Job Function	
11:30							
12:00	Stress Mgt.	Stress Mgt.	Stress Mgt.	Stress Mgt.	Stress Mgt.	Stress Mgt.	Lunch
12:30	Lunch	Lunch	Lunch	Lunch	Lunch	Lunch	
1:00	Group Process	Group Process	NA Steps	Group Process	Big Book/	Recreation	AA/Al-Anon
1:30					Group Lecture	Visitors	
2:00	AA Big Book	AA Big Book	Film	Na Big book	Steps		
2:30							

Time							
3:00 3:30	Recreation	Recreation	Recreation	Recreation	Recreation		Film
4:00 4:30		Women's Grp.			Going Home		
5:00 5:30	Dinner School*	Dinner School*	Dinner School*	Dinner School*	Dinner School*		Dinner
6:00 6:30						AA/NA Orientation Group Feedback	Family Process
7:00 7:30						Rec. Movie	
8:00 8:30	Counseling Exercise	Supervised Study	Supervised Recreation	Supervised Recreation	Supervised Recreation		Supervised Study
9:00 9:30	Snacks	Snacks	Snacks	Snacks	Snacks	Snacks	Snacks
10:00	Bedtime	Bedtime	Bedtime	Bedtime	Bedtime	Bedtime	Bedtime
10:30	Lights out	Lights out	Lights out	Lights out	Lights out	Lights out	Lights out

*Supervised Activities replace school during summer months.

As you can see, there's little time for kids to hang out. The day is highly structured and moves smoothly from one activity to the next. There is a routine to each day, with emphasis on group therapy and AA involvement.

After getting out of a ten-week residential rehab, Trish went directly to a program of extended care. For a minimum of one month, from 8 a.m. to 5 p.m., Trish carried on a similiar routine of alcohol education, group and individual counseling, and AA meetings.

"I really needed aftercare. No way was I ready to go back to my school. It was hard enough going back to my family," Trish said. "I needed help getting back into my family routine before facing school and my friends again. My ex-friends, I should say."

The goals of an aftercare program are:

• Continued sobriety;
• Participation in AA's 12-step recovery program;
• Adjustment to reentry into family life through counseling;
• Development of more self-awareness and social skills;
• Learning of recreational alternatives to alcohol such as sports (running, weight lifting, volleyball, canoeing, swimming) and therapeutically creative activities such as art, music, woodworking;
• Vocational training and job skills;
• Education through tutoring;
• Establishment of a network of support people who are also recovering.

After Trish's month of aftercare, she and her family attended Tuesday night and Saturday morning groups for another four months.

"Rehab turned out to be harder than I ever imagined it would be," said Trish. "But then again I was never sober enough even to imagine doing it. I learned a lot. It was painful and scary, and there were times when all I wanted to do was run away so I could get a drink. But now that I've been sober for six months, six very long, hard months, I'm glad I did it. Otherwise I'd probably be dead or something by now. That's just the way it is."

CHAPTER 16

Alcoholics

Anonymous

F or those of you who think that your drinking is starting to cause problems and interfere with your life . . .

For those of you who have lost control over your drinking . . .

For those of you who are now being controlled by your drinking . . .

Help comes to many through the AA program. Alcoholics Anonymous are people, from as young as eight or nine to those in their seventies and older, who have admitted that alcohol has control over them.

Alcoholics Anonymous is an international fellowship of people in 134 countries who have one purpose—to stay sober themselves and help others who turn to them achieve sobriety.

Kids, teens, women, men, parents, grandparents, all races, all backgrounds, all religions, all social levels, rich, poor, white, black, red, and more belong to AA.

You don't need to have been a skid row bum to go to AA. Some were. You don't have to have been jailed, fined, or lost your license for drunk driving to join AA. Some members have. You don't have to have committed crimes against others such as your family, society, your boss, or yourself to attend AA meetings. Some have. All you have to do is know that alcohol is an influence in your life.

Many kids are surprised to have AA suggested to them as a help in dealing with alcohol abuse.

"I'm too young to be an alcoholic."

"Isn't that for rip-roaring, falling-down drunks? I'm not like that."

"I don't black out or have memory lapses. I'm just flunking some classes in school. I don't think AA can do anything about that."

"AA is for *real* alcoholics. Like people drinking for years. I haven't been drinking that long; less than a year maybe."

Kids are asked to try some AA meetings, just to go and listen to what is said there. You can go back to drinking if that's your choice. There's no high-pressure push to be a member.

But if you feel sometimes that your drinking is affecting you inside, in your body and heart and mind, AA may just help. You are the only one who can judge whether you are abusing alcohol and have a drinking problem. No one can make you believe that except you. But if alcohol is interfering in your life, if you've been guilty or ashamed of your drinking, this may be the place to get you on the road to a new beginning.

AA members go to meetings as often as they can. Meetings are held in churches, hospitals, rented rooms, all over. It's not hard to find meetings where you live. Your school guidance counselor or substance abuse counselor, your minister, priest, rabbi, the phone book, and your local AA organization can all help you find out when and where the meetings are. That's not a problem. Deciding to go is the first big step.

At the meetings you'll hear people talking about their lives and how drinking interfered in their lives. As you hear those stories, you might recognize something about yourself. Tuning in to the feelings of the person speaking sometimes sets off a bell in your head and heart. "Hey, that's me too!"

You might not get much out of the first meetings. Try to attend a few. Find out where and when the teen meetings are held so you won't feel so different. Maybe you'll decide to keep on drinking. Maybe the words you hear at a meeting or two will stay with you so that later on you'll come back for a few more meetings.

AA members work on changing themselves on day at a time. You don't have to solemnly swear not to touch a drop of liquor for the rest of your life. AA is more realistic than that. Some members tried those pledges and maybe did stay sober for one day, one week, one month, one year, but they drank again.

AA members focus on staying sober now, this one day. TODAY. "For the next twenty-four hours I will not take a drink. Maybe tomorrow I'll be tempted to, but not today." Today is the only important day. You can't change yesterday, and tomorrow never comes. It becomes today and you'll focus on staying sober today.

AA meetings are of several kinds. Open meetings are for anyone who wants to go: alcoholics and nonalcoholics, community members, families of alcoholics, and anyone who wants to attend. The only obligation is not telling the names of the AA members outside the meeting.

At an open meeting a leader begins the meeting and introduces the speakers. Usually the speakers are AA members who talk about their drinking experiences and how they joined AA. You can get information about the recovery program and how AA works. Usually there are light refreshments and some socializing.

A closed meeting involves the members of a particular AA group and visiting members. Suppose you were in a teen AA group in your hometown. If you felt the need or wish to attend a meeting when you were in another state visiting your grandparents for the summer, you could find a teen group there. You'd be welcome.

The closed meeting provides an opportunity for members to talk about their own personal phases of alcoholism that are best understood by other alcoholics. Newcomers may find the closed meetings valuable for asking questions and getting clarification of things they need to explore.

There are no requirements about attending meetings. Some newcomers want to attend every night. Others find once a week is enough.

There are evening meetings, morning meetings, lunchtime and afternoon meetings. Once you open the door for yourself to see if AA can help you with your alcohol problem, the members *want* to reach out to help you.

In AA no one *has* to do anything. It is all up to you. Many members attend meetings frequently because in addition to helping themselves stay sober for this one day, they are reaching out and helping others achieve sobriety too. Helping others makes you feel good about yourself, and that usually keeps you coming back to do more.

Increasing your self-esteem and lending strength to others in need sometimes is the push that will get you over a problem in your own life.

But that sounds as if I'll be spending a big part of my life going to meetings, you say. True, achieving sobriety and maintaining it will take time out of your day. But when you drank, how many hours, days, weekends, or even weeks did you "lose"? You can't hurry this process. It won't be that you'll go to meetings for two weeks and be "cured." People who have the illness of alcoholism are never "cured." They can arrest or stop the disease, but if they start drinking again it will be out of control again. Most authorities on alcoholism maintain that an alcoholic can never drink again because there is no "normal" drinking for an alcoholic.

If the AA program is to help you achieve and maintain sobriety, you need to admit that you have a problem with alcohol and that you cannot drink normally again. *You must have the desire to stop drinking.*

Here are some kids who joined AA because their drinking was out of control:

Dana was fifteen when she went to her first AA meeting.

"I got into drinking the way most kids do, you know, a couple of parties, drinking on weekends, someone brings a pint to school and we sneak it at lunch. I was kinda chubby in junior high, so I pretended to go on liquid diets to lose weight.

"The beer and the pints of rum that we hid in our lockers actually made me gain weight. Then I hated myself even more. Yuck, I was fat and ugly and didn't have a boyfriend. When I went to parties, I would get into the chugging contests with the boys and they would cheer me on. It was the only time anyone ever really paid attention to me, and

I liked it. It made me feel skinny, and pretty, and popular.

"One day after drinking at lunchtime, my two best friends and I got caught in the school bathroom. My one friend was throwing up. I think she was still hung over from the night before.

"We were sent to the principal's office and my friends turned *me* in! They told him I was the one who brought the bottles to school all the time and that this was their first time—that's why Mandy was throwing up. I was so shocked at my so-called friends that I didn't even bother to defend myself. Plus I was pretty drunk, and I didn't want him to know how much by my slurred speech.

"My parents must have suspected my drinking because they took me to our family doctor after I sobered up. We've known this doctor since I was a baby, and he talked to me, really talked, and for the first time I started to listen to someone about alcohol. I had always tuned out the classes we had on alcohol and drugs—thought it was all pretty stupid. I mean, I liked to drink. I *loved* the way it made me feel. Then I realized that I had to do something about it before things got worse.

"I went to my first AA meeting with my mother. There were all kinds of people there, but I was too scared to talk to anyone. They were all friendly and nice to Mom and me. I tried to act as if my mother was the one with the problem, not I. Neither of us said anything. We just listened. Mom said she'd drive me to every meeting I wanted to go to, but that it had to be I who wanted to go and do something about my drinking.

"At first, I didn't want to hear that word 'alcoholic'. Man, I never thought I'd be an alcoholic. It's hard to admit. The most helpful were the meetings for the kids my age. It was hard for me to tune in to a sixty-year-old grandmother

who drank because she was all alone. But the kids' meetings helped. There was even a ten-year-old. Can you
imagine that? Now I can.

"That was the beginning. It was hard getting better and
staying sober. That one day at a time thing helps. I can't
worry about tomorrow, just today. Don't drink today.
Keep away from that first drink today. Because if I take
that first drink, I know that I won't stop. I'm an alcoholic."

Michael, seventeen, tells about his experience.

"I was a big-shot athlete and never figured that my
drinking would mess me up. I mean I didn't do what some
of the other guys were doing—no pot, no cocaine, no
crack. Only drinking. I didn't think that was so bad.

"I didn't even notice when I went from just drinking
beer and a few shots of whiskey to drinking whatever I
could get my hands on. I stole liquor from my parents'
cabinet and filled the bottles with water. Dad asked me
about it a few times—I guess he could taste the difference—
but I blamed my sister's boyfriend and got them in a lot of
trouble.

"I didn't even pay much attention when I started doing
all that lying to cover up for my drinking. I would throw
up some mornings, and my mother was worried that I
had a food allergy or that the coach was working us too
hard to put on weight or take weight off.

"I guess the turning point was when I was real nervous
about this county tournament wrestling match. I had to
drop down to the lower weight class, and I did it by not
eating and trying not to drink much. I wanted to be pretty
sober because I was up against one of my rivals.

"But I got nervous and gulped down some vodka and

some bourbon I had hidden in my gym bag. I could feel it go through my body like a hot rush. I got a burst of energy and went out to meet my opponent.

"Right away I could tell he was stronger and in control. The rush was wearing off, and I felt light-headed and drunk. He even said under his breath out there in the middle of the mat, 'You smell like a brewery!' And I guess I did. I could see my parents cheering for me, and the coach was screaming at me to make some of my moves, but I sort of melted away and everything got real fuzzy.

"Then I got pinned and the other guy jumped up off me and the ref raised his hand as the winner. I couldn't even stand up. I could see the coach shaking his head and looking disgusted at me, and all I could do was roll over onto my stomach and start throwing up. I threw up and threw up right out there in front of the whole gym filled with people, until I started throwing up blood.

"I could hear Mom screaming at Coach something like, '*You* did this to him—making him lose all that weight. *You* made him sick!' Then I passed out and woke up in the hospital.

"Mom was still going on about how she was going to make sure Coach lost his job because of what he did to me. Dad just looked me in the eye and asked if that was the truth—that I got sick from dropping weight and all the wrestling pressure. I couldn't answer him. All I could do was cry. I felt like a baby, but I finally told them that I drank. That I drank a lot and for a long time, I told them I needed help.

"I went to my first AA meeting there at the hospital. I was moved to a detox unit and started my recovery right there. Leaving the hospital was hard. I didn't want to go home or to school or to face my friends and especially the coach. I had to face disciplinary action for going to a school event drunk and was suspended from the team. I could see how alcohol had really wrecked my life, that I had really wrecked my life. But AA helped me to go on and admit that I needed help, that I was powerless over alcohol, and that I could work the program to get sober and stay sober.

"That first year was really tough. Lots of times I wanted a drink, but I kept thinking that I only had to stay sober until I fell asleep at night. Today. I would go to meetings sometimes twice in one day or call another member when I really wanted to drink. They understood because they had been through the same thing, the same feelings. Even though their lives were different from mine, the feelings were the same.

"I have to thank my parents for sticking by me. After Mom calmed down from the shock, she was supportive. Dad was great. You know, he told me that his father, my grandfather, was a big drinker and that he had noticed some of the same things in me. I guess he didn't want to think that his only son, the big jock, was a drunk.

"I was allowed back on the team the next season. And I also helped start an AA group right in my school. Everyone had seen me at that match, so it was no secret after a while that I was an alcoholic. So I used that to help a few other kids.

"Not too many kids were willing to join at first. Kids would call me Reverend and put me down when I talked about the dangers of drinking. It was hard to take, but through the program I was able to face it and do something positive with it rather than give up and start drinking again.

"I'm not glad I went through all of this. I wish I hadn't hurt my parents and my coach so much, but it happened and I can't change yesterday. Today. That's all I think about now, I'm sober today."

Marti doesn't want to dwell on her past life of drinking. She concentrates on who she is right now—a sober seventeen-year-old.

"It took me a long time to get the AA message, but when I finally faced my loss of control over my drinking, I wised up. At AA they gave me some simple slogans to remember when I felt down and wanted a drink. 'One Day at a Time' helps me to keep on working on today. Yesterday is over and tomorrow's not here. Today. That's the key. Today.

"Another slogan I like is 'Easy Does It' because I am always very intense about things. I definitely got intense about my drinking. But I've learned through AA to go easy on myself. I can face today, and that's all I'm working on at the moment.

"The twelve-step program was hard for me at first, but as I went to the suggested ninety meetings in ninety days it made more sense. Now I use those twelve steps sort of as rules for my life. They have helped keep me from drinking again, and my life is on the upswing. I used to think I would die before I was eighteen. Now I can look forward to a future. Without AA I don't think I would have made it."

These are kids just like you and everyone who sits in your English class every day. They spent days, weeks, months, and even years drinking. They all reached a point where alcohol was out of control in their life, and they were able to do something about it. The "something" they found was Alcoholics Anoymous—a group of people who had been right where they were and had come back from that never-never land.

They found sobriety and a new way to live their lives without drinking. They asked for help. You can too.

Following are the twelve steps of the Alcoholics Anonymous program:

THE TWELVE STEPS OF
ALCOHOLICS ANONYMOUS

1. We admitted we were powerless over alcohol—that our lives had become unmanageable.
2. Came to believe that a Power greater than ourselves could restore us to sanity.
3. Made a decision to turn our will and our lives over to the care of God *as we understood Him.*
4. Made a searching and fearless moral inventory of ourselves.
5. Admitted to God, to ourselves and to another human being the exact nature of our wrongs.
6. Were entirely ready to have God remove all these defects of character.
7. Humbly asked Him to remove our short comings.
8. Made a list of all persons we had harmed, and became willing to make amends to them all.
9. Made direct amends to such people wherever possible, except when to do so would injure them or others.
10. Continued to take personal inventory and when we were wrong promptly admitted it.
11. Sought through prayer and meditation to improve our conscious contact with God, *as we understood Him,* praying only for knowledge of His will for us and the power to carry that out.

12. Having had a spiritual awakening as the result of these steps, we tried to carry this message to alcoholics, and to practice these principles in all our affairs.

CHAPTER ◇ 17

Recovery

Recovery. That word usually means that you have gotten over whatever ailed you. For alcoholics recovery is a lifetime process.

"I know now that I can't ever take another drink," said Matthew, a recovering seventeen-year-old alcoholic. "If I start again, I won't be able to stop myself, and this time I might die."

Recovery. For others that word means getting over something and looking toward the future.

"I never thought I would make it to eighteen," Kelly said. "When I was at my worst, right before the car crash that killed my best friend, I was sure I'd be dead by now. It sure is a different feeling to look forward—to graduation, to college even. Can you believe that? Me, in college? I never could. Not until now. I'm recovering from life in the darkest pit I could have dug for myself."

Teens who are recovering come out of rehabilitation clinics, hospitals, and counseling programs with a new set of rules for their lives. Many of them had lived by no rules for a number of years. The only thing that mattered in their lives was alcohol: how they could keep the supply coming, how much they could drink, how much money it took to keep them in liquor, and how to keep drinking so they didn't have to face the "real" world.

Said Pete, sixteen, "The rehab counselors stressed that when we got out and returned home we *had* to change our people, places, and things in order to stay sober and straight. That's really hard sometimes. So hard that a few times I just wanted to go back to rehab; I knew what to expect there, but out here I was really scared of what could happen."

Changing *people, places,* and *things.* When you are in the same neighborhood and the same school where all your problems happened, changing your *people,* namely your friends, is hard. They will seek you out. "Hey, I got a bottle stashed in my locker. Meet me out by the football bleachers third period like we always did," comes at you when you least expect it. How do you say no when you always said yes?

"What's the matter? You chicken? You stuck up now and too good for us? We'll pick you up after school, and you better have the stuff for us like you always did. I don't care where you've been. You're back." Scary to resist this kind of pressure, isn't it?

Those kids with whom you used to get high are still doing it. They don't want you to change. They want you to stay exactly the way they are—drunk, high, messing up, in trouble, kicked out of school and home. When they see you straight, it may bother them that you are getting it together, which reminds them that they are not. They may resent you for what you've done and want to bring you back down to where they are. That's much more comfortable for them.

"My parents wanted me to change schools and go live with my aunt," said Stacy, fourteen. "But I felt that was not really facing my problems, you know? I was in rehab for three months. It was a time I never want to go through again. It was hard, but now that I'm on this side of it, I know I needed it. But if I don't change from my old friends, and just move away, you know? Then I'm avoiding what I really need to do to be strong in not drinking again."

Sometimes it comes down to forcing yourself to make new friends or stay a loner for a while to live down your reputation in your school or town. Some of the kids you want to be friends with now may not know where you're coming from. After all, a few months ago you were one of the ones from whom their parents told them to keep away. You have to earn trust and be visible as a sober person.

"For a long time the only other kids I hung around with were other recovering alcoholics. We had a strong school program, and they ran a teen AA group right in school every Wednesday after school," Kirk said.

"At first when I came out of rehab I went to an aftercare program every day after school and on Saturdays. As long as I made it through the school day, I could get to aftercare, which helped me survive those first weeks home. Then I got hooked up with my school AA program, and they were the only friends I had for a few months.

"Now finally, after seven months out of rehab and sober for nine months, I have made a friend who is not connected with any program. He's just my friend. I feel I've come a long way."

And he has. Facing your old drinking crowd, going to parties again where you used to get wasted and now you sip soda, and not returning those phone calls that you know mean pressure from drinking friends takes strength, courage, and willpower. You can have help and encouragement through all these adjustments, but you are the one who has to live it.

Changing *places*. Avoiding your old drinking places means finding new hangouts. Not going to the second-floor boys bathroom after English class to sneak a swig means rerouting your walks in the school halls.

If Stephanie's house is where everyone goes on Saturday nights, it may mean going bowling with your sister instead of drinking at Stephanie's. Change your places. Avoiding old temptations and creating new places to go takes direction. You can get help with choosing that direction, but you take those steps for the rest of your sober life.

Change your *things*. The games you play, the toys you play with, the things that are important to you and have meaning in your life are very different now. Whereas a bottle used to be the most important "thing" in your life— or the emergency six-pack hidden in the trunk of your car or under your shoes—now something must repace those things.

For Lenore, it was trophies that she started winning in five-mile runs. "I needed something to do to fill in all the time that I used to spend drunk, so I started jogging. That really helped me to let off some stress, got me in shape, and helped me to feel good about myself little by little. I ran this first race and won a second-place trophy! I think there were only four girls my age in the race, so even if I had come in last I would have been fourth, but that trophy did something to me. I had never won anything before in my life!"

That trophy told Lenore something—that she was a winner and that she could accomplish something. Everything and anything you can do to boost your self-esteem during recovery and sobriety will move you further ahead and away from your old habits.

For Keith, photography replaced his old "thing" (alcohol) with a new thing that he could enjoy.

"I feel I missed so much when I drank for those two years," said Keith, seventeen, "I started taking pictures of my family, trying to give back to them after I had taken so much away. Then I took photos of my friends at our AA activities—when we went to the beach or to the museum. They liked their 'sober' pictures. Their families hadn't taken many pictures of them when they were drinking and causing problems."

When you are drinking enough to be a heavy abuser or an alcoholic, you lose touch with all the "things" that used to bring you pleasure. Alcohol became the "thing" that seemed to bring you pleasure at first but then brought a whole lot of pain too. Replace that pain with some positive "thing"—something that will give you pride in yourself.

Changing people, places, and things are very important steps in staying sober and recovering from a destructive time of your life. You can get loads of help and support in making these changes. But the most important aspect is that *you* have to want to do it. No one can do it for you. It's not that simple. But *you can do it*!

AUTOBIOGRAPHY IN FIVE SHORT CHAPTERS
by Portia Nelson

I

I walk, down the street.
    There is a deep hole in the sidewalk.
    I fall in
    I am lost . . . I am helpless
        It isn't my fault.
It takes forever to find a way out.

II

I walk down the same street.
There is a deep hole in the sidewalk.
I pretend I don't see it.
I fall in again.
I can't believe I am in the same place.
but it isn't my fault.
It still takes a long time to get out.

III

I walk down the same street.
There is a deep hole in the sidewalk.
I see it is there.
I still fall in . . . it's a habit.
my eyes are open.
I know where I am.
It is my fault.
I get out immediately.

IV

I walk down the same street.
There is a deep hole in the sidewalk.
I walk around it.

V

I walk down another street.

From *Repeat After Me*, by Claudia Black.

CHAPTER 18

Iron Eyes Cody

Many people—adults, teens, preteens, yes, even children—make choices about drinking.

You will make many decisions about alcohol in the course of your lifetime. When you get caught up in each new decision, each new situation in which you must decide whether or not to drink or how much to drink, keep the following story in mind. The author is Iron Eyes Cody, a motion picture and TV star.

On film in Hollywood I have played many American Indian roles—the warrior, the medicine man, the chief wearing his double-tailed eagle headdress and smoking the pipe of peace.

And in a TV spot for the "Keep America Beautiful" campaign, I was an Indian drifting alone in a canoe. As I saw how our waters were being polluted, a single tear rolled down my cheek, telling the whole story. All three versions of my public-service "tear" commercial are still on TV after seventeen years. But now I have another story to tell, an old legend, with a warning as potent as that tear.

Many years ago, Indian youths would go away in solitude to prepare for manhood. One such youth hiked into a beautiful valley, green with trees, bright with flowers. There he fasted. But on the third day, as he looked up at the surrounding mountains, he noticed one tall rugged peak, capped with dazzling snow.

I will test myself against that mountain, he thought. He put on his buffalo-hide shirt, threw his blanket over his shoulders and set off to climb the peak.

When he reached the top he stood on the rim of the world. He could see forever, and his heart swelled with pride. Then he heard a rustle at his feet, and looking down, he saw a snake. Before he could move, the snake spoke:

"I am about to die," said the snake. "It is too cold up here and I am freezing. There is no food and I am starving. Put me under your shirt and take me down to the valley."

"No," said the youth. "I am forewarned. I know your kind. You are a rattlesnake. If I pick you up, you will bite, and your bite will kill me."

"Not so," said the snake. "I will treat you differently. If you do this for me, you will be special. I will not harm you."

The youth resisted for a while, but this was a very persuasive snake with beautiful markings. At last the youth tucked it under his shirt and carried it down to the valley. There he laid it gently on the grass, when suddenly the snake coiled, rattled, and leapt, biting him on the leg.

"But you promised—"cried the youth.

"You knew what I was when you picked me up," said the snake as it slithered away.

And now, wherever I go, I tell that story. I tell it especially to the young people of this nation who might be tempted by drugs. I want them to remember the words of the snake: *You knew what I was when you picked me up.**

Many school systems begin teaching about alcohol and other drug use as early as first, second, and third grades.

You knew what I was when you picked me up.

Middle schools and junior highs all over this country take specific time within their curriculum to drive home the information about the dangers of alcohol and drug use.

You knew what I was when you picked me up.

High schools incorporate alcohol and drug education in almost every aspect of the student's school life.

You knew what I was when you picked me up.

Probably 99 percent of alcoholics and other drug addicts started with drinking that first beer or glass of wine and smoking that first cigarette.

You knew what I was when you picked me up.

Some kids live with the problem of having one or two alcoholic parents. Yet they go out and get drunk to "forget" their troubles.

You knew what I was when you picked me up.

Feeling good about yourself, being popular in school or at parties, having friends, and enjoying your life does not come from a bottle. It comes from your own self-esteem. Self-esteem happens when you believe in yourself, love yourself, and can be proud of yourself for your life. That doesn't come from a can of beer or a bottle of scotch.

You knew what I was when you picked me up.

Your friends may offer you alcohol and even pressure

---

*Reprinted with permission from Guidepost Magazine, © 1988 by Guidepost Associates, Inc., Carmel, N.Y.

you to drink with them or they won't be your "friend" anymore.

You knew what I was when you picked me up.

If you are lonely, sad, depressed, and feel really lousy about your life right now, get help from understanding counselors, parents, or sober friends. Help doesn't come in a six-pack.

You knew what I was when you picked me up.

Commercials and magazine ads, videos, TV shows, and movies paint wonderful, funny pictures of partying and drinking. It's fun! It makes you popular! You'll feel great and forget your troubles! You will have romance and love if you drink with your date, boyfriend, girlfriend! Drinking will make you *cool*! Promises, promises, promises. Lies, lies, lies.

You knew what I was when you picked me up.

You will meet the opportunity to make the decision to drink or not many, many times in your life.

Remember Iron Eyes Cody and the wisdom of the snake legend:

You knew what I was when you picked me up.

Appendix

Addresses, information, and resources

Alcoholics Anonymous World Services, Inc.
P.O. Box 459, Grand Central Station
New York, NY 10163

Al-Anon Family Group Headquarters, Inc.
P.O. Box 182, Madison Square Station
New York, NY 10159-0182

Alateen
P.O. Box 182, Madison Square Station
New York, NY 10159-0182

Alcohol and Drug Problems Association of North America, Inc.
  (ADPA)
444 North Capitol Street NW
Washington, DC 20001

National Clearinghouse for Alcohol Information
U.S. Department of Health and Human Services
P.O. Box 2345
Rockville, MD 20852

National Institute on Alcohol Abuse and Alcoholism
5600 Fishers lane
Rockville, MD 20857

Places to go for information

Local chapters of Alcoholics Anonymous (AA), Alateen, and Al-Anon

State department for Alcohol Beverage Control (ABC)

Local health department

Local hospital alcohol program

Your school district's alcohol and substance abuse counselor

Your middle or high school guidance department

Your health teacher

Bibliography

Books

American Automobile Association. *Teacher's Guide to Alcohol Countermeasures*, Falls Church, VA: AAA, 1976.

Black, Claudia, PhD. *It Will Never Happen to Me.* Denver; M.A.C. Printing & Publications Division, 1981.

———. *Repeat After Me.* Denver: M.A.C. Printing & Publications Division, 1985.

Claypool, Jane. *Alcohol and You.* New York: Franklin Watts, 1981.

Englebardt, Stanley L. *Kids and Alcohol, The Deadliest Drug.* New York: Lothrop, Lee, & Shephard Company, 1975.

Fishman, Ross, PhD. *Alcohol and Alcoholism, The Encyclopedia of Psychoactive Drugs*, New York: Chelsea House Publishers, 1986.

Howard, Marion. *Did I Have a Good Time?* New York: The Continuum Publishing Corporation, 1980.

Lang, Alan, PhD. *Alcohol and Teenage Drinking.* New York: Chelsea House Publishers, 1985.

Langone, John. *Bombed, Buzzed, Smashed, or Sober.* New York: Avon Books, 1976.

Milam, Dr. James, and Katherine Ketcham. *Under the Influence.* New York: Bantam Books, 1985.

Milgram, Dr. Gail. *Coping With Alcohol.* New York: Rosen Publishing Group, 1985.

Newman, Sandy. *You Can Say No to a Drink or a Drug—What Every Kid Should Know.* New York: Putnam Publishing Group, Perigee Books, 1986.

Stearn, Marshall B., PhD. *Drinking and Driving, Know Your Limits and Liabilities*. Sausalito, CA: Park West Publishing Co., 1985.

Pamphlets and Articles

"What Every Kid Should Know About Alcohol." South Deerfield, MA: Channing L. Bete Co., Inc., 1982.

Alcoholics Anonymous. "This Is AA." New York: Alcoholics Anonymous World Services, Inc., 1984.

———. "Young People and AA." New York: Alcoholics Anonymous World Services, Inc., 1989.

Conover, Kirsten A. "Hammered: Alcohol Plagues Teens." *Christian Science Monitor*, 1988.

Milgram, Dr. Gail, "What Is Alcohol? And Why Do People Drink?" New Brunswick, NJ: Rutgers University Press, 1988.

Schafer, Connie, "Student Assistance Programs Follow Lead of Industry's EAPs." American Association for Counseling and Development, *Guidepost*, Sept. 21, 1989.

Index